Showdown at Lost Pass

SHOWDOWN AT LOST PASS
Robert H. Redding

When the harsh winter of '86-'87 wipes out his ranch, Keely McGuire takes to the road. He's not quite sure what he's looking for until he comes upon the Mossman place. There, working and living with Cy Mossman and his family, Keely finds the warm feeling of home. And in the eyes of Marcy, Mossman's beautiful daughter, he finds the only future he'll ever want.

But nearby live the greedy Clatchett brothers, who will stop at nothing to get Mossman's land, and they achieve their end through the vilest of crimes, making it look like Keely was responsible. Keely must flee for his life, but he vows revenge. In the forest, Josh Deerface, an Indian fleeing from an enemy tribe, and Tanada, a beautiful young outcast, join forces with him. Together they are able to tame the wilderness. But will they be able to withstand the forces of evil that are closing in upon them as the Clatchett brothers begin their relentless advance?

Other Avalon Books by Robert H. Redding

LOCK'S REVENGE

SHOWDOWN
AT
LOST PASS

Robert H. Redding

AVALON BOOKS
THOMAS BOUREGY AND COMPANY, INC.
401 LAFAYETTE STREET
NEW YORK, NEW YORK 10003

PRINTED IN THE UNITED STATES OF AMERICA
BY HADDON CRAFTSMEN, SCRANTON, PENNSYLVANIA

Chapter One

The terrible winter of 1886–87 was finally overcome by the warming
winds of spring, but the shortgrass country
of the Great Plains lay dead under dirty
snow. Far into the distance, Keely
McGuire's unwilling eyes saw cattle that
had died in the blizzards. They were *his*
cattle. They had made up the backbone of
his ranch, the KM. He had lost over three-
quarters of his small herd, and the survi-
vors were skin, bone, and tail. Once, the
cattle had been his life, but now his life
was finished.

Lifeless hooves stuck up through the
snow like dull beacons under the yellow
sun. Brown hides returned the sun's rays
with the slick, glossy sheen of death.
Sightless eyes gazed into eternity. Keely

1

McGuire's dream had crashed to the depths like an avalanche.

He had bought the ranch five years ago, when he was an innocent fellow of twenty-four—innocent in many ways, but not in the ways of handling cattle. Keely knew about cattle. He'd been raised on a ranch in Texas, but he'd been innocent in the ways of weather. For five years he'd fought the Northern winters, and each winter he had lost some of his herd to cold and blizzards. Wyoming cold didn't exist where he came from; neither did those kinds of blizzards. Each year he had lost cattle, but each year he had managed to recoup his losses and even make a small profit. The ranch had not been a huge success, but it had been alive and kicking.

As Keely surveyed the scene of desolation that stretched to the horizon like some kind of hell, he knew that this year he'd lost too much. He could never recover as he had before. He didn't even want to try. He was sickened by the carnage, by winter's cruel joke. A man worked all summer in the dry, parched heat to build his herd. Then winter took it away. It was time to try something else. Or, perhaps, to do nothing at all. He was weary of responsibility. Maybe he'd hit the trail and let life open up to him again, one day at a time.

He wasn't broke. He had a little money from the sale of the best of the surviving cattle. With a heavy sigh Keely turned his horse, Thorny, back toward the ranch. Thorny stepped carefully, avoiding the bodies of cattle that had once promised many dollars per head at the pens. Keely felt a twinge of guilt over his self-pity. He wasn't the only one who had been hurt. Many ranches across the upper Plains Country had grappled with nature that year and lost. Nearly all of the outfits were larger than his. If the big ranchers couldn't make it, he needn't be ashamed of his own loss.

Keely was more sorrowed than anything else. A large shadow had settled over his usually open nature. Lean and leather-hard from working at one of the hardest and most dangerous jobs a man could find, he had become tough. His gray eyes glinted in the soft sunlight. They reflected some of the spirit that had enabled him to remain a cowboy-rancher, but there was sadness at the edges.

He banged a fist into an open hand, and the sound made Thorny's ears twitch. Those poor cattle! While the winds had whipped and thrown frozen snow at them a hundred miles an hour, there had been nothing he could do to help. While the cold had turned their blood to ice, some dying on their feet, he had hunkered by the stove, unable to do anything. He had raged. A man could fight another man. He could use his fists on another man or draw a gun, but he couldn't fight nature. Nature was the eternal champion, and all a man could do was crouch by the stove and listen to the demented wind kill his critters. All a man could do was feed the stabled horses and his own face, and rage helplessly.

When, after months, the wind called off its ice-sabred armies, a silence came over the land. It was a silence that settled over the entire country, the silence of a tomb.

Perhaps it was the great, stony silence that moved Keely most. It was spring. Calves should be aborning, roundups should be taking place. Cows should be bawling for lost young 'uns, and young 'uns should be bawling when hot branding irons pressed into their flesh. The ranches should be crackling with men and their comings and goings, with their doing of the things that made cattle operations successful.

There was none of that now. There was only the graveyard silence in which no life moved. Keely allowed himself a grim smile. It would be a mighty spooky moment if life suddenly arose from the ghostly prairie. But that could happen only in one of those weird stories by Edgar Allan Poe. He sometimes read them to pass the time. It wasn't exactly reading to cheer a man, but Poe was the only author he had at home.

When he reached the ranch house, three men were waiting for him. They were all that was left of his crew, and he'd kept them on just in case some kind of recovery was possible. Even though he'd sold off the most vigorous of his remaining cattle, a man hated to give up. The three men had waited while he took one last hard look at his property.

"So?" The questioner was Curly. That was all Keely knew him by, and that was because the man had curly hair.

"You saw it," Keely said.

"Yep."

"We stayin' or not?" This was from Blacky, who had a black beard.

"We're closing up, boys."

"Dang!" muttered a third, called Baldy for obvious reasons.

Keely rarely knew the full names of his cowboys. As the saying went, "All a man needs is a handle to grab on to," and that was all most of his cowboys ever gave.

"Kind of figured that," Curly said, "but we was hopin', you know."

Keely nodded, then said, "I owe you each a month's pay. Come to the office."

The four men tramped into the main house's front room, where Keely went to his desk. He peeled some bills from a roll and then counted out some coins. The men took what was offered with satisfaction.

"You need me again," Curly said, "I'll be around these parts."

Keely accepted the offer with a warm handshake. Curly was a good cowboy and a good man.

"Same with me," Blacky said. "You always got the best cooks here at the KM."

Keely grinned. "You bean-grinders! Never had better grub-snatchers than you. Well, it'll be restaurant food for all of us for a while."

"Restaurants," Baldy grumbled. "Garbage."

"Ham and eggs can cost twenty-five cents," Blacky said. "Heck, I don't want to buy the stove, just eats."

The three men shook Keely's hand and left. Moments later he heard their horses break into a canter toward Gunny, the regional railhead. Chances were that the three would find work. They were all top hands, with solid reputations in the country. The saying went, "A man's reputation goes first, and all he has to do is follow."

Keely went next to the cook's quarters and paid him. He was an extremely thin man, with the inevitable handle of Skinny. His eyes were somber.

"What you goin' to do?" he asked as he tucked his pay into a shirt pocket.

"Don't know yet."

"Ramble around, mebbe?"

"Maybe."

"Well, good luck, boss. Don't take any wooden nickels."

Skinny made an attempt at a laugh, failed, shook his head, and departed. "If you ever need me, just holler," he muttered.

Keely didn't drink much, but he kept a bottle in a desk drawer. He poured half a tumbler for himself. Then, sipping the whiskey, he moved slowly through the house. It was still fully furnished, but there was nobody to sell the furnishings to. It was sturdy stuff, oak, a lot of it, and if he ever returned, it would be as good and serviceable as now.

He visited all the rooms, and the big bedroom held a special poignancy. He had hoped that one day there would be a wife for him, and then children, and the big bedroom would belong to him and his wife. His children would have their own rooms, for he had built the house on a large scale. That dream was over. Savage winds had blown it away. There were women in Gunny, good women who had frontier experience and knew about the hardships of ranching life, and one of them would have been right for the KM. But the KM was gone, and the dream, no more substantial than a candle flame, had been snuffed out.

Keely returned to the kitchen. He poured the rest of his drink down the sink and washed the glass. Then he went out on the front porch, picking up a sign along the way. The sign's message was: *Help yourself, just don't burn the place down.* He nailed the sign to the door. Drifters might want a place for a night or two. There was little sense in locking the door. If anybody wanted to come in, he'd break in, anyway.

Next, Keely threw his saddlebags across Thorny's broad back and mounted him. Sensing his master's gloom, Thorny was docile. Ordinarily, he might have kicked up a fuss just for the heck of it, but he walked quietly to the edge of the compound, where he felt his boss turn in the saddle to look back. He didn't see the man give a long, slow salute, but he felt the gentle tap of spurs.

"Let's get going, fella," came the familiar voice, and Thorny set off at a trot.

Keely set a westward course, steering away from Gunny. The place was too sad for him right now. It wasn't that he couldn't take it, but why add more grief?

Gunny was shadowed with faces as grim as his own. They belonged to ranchers who had gone bust just as he had and were waiting for the train to take them someplace else. They didn't care where else, just anywhere out of shortgrass country. Keely knew most of them and they were friends. They had all gabbed repeatedly about their futures in recent weeks, so there was no use in going over the whole thing again. Keely McGuire cared for his friends, but there was nothing he could do for them—any more than there was anything they could do for him. Every man must face his destiny alone. So he kept clear, and rode west.

After several weeks of wandering he became aware of a strange feeling. He felt as though he were a bubble floating in the air. It was not a good feeling. He hadn't expected it, and it seemed that having no place to hang your hat wasn't as great as some made it out to be. He'd always heard that having the sky for a roof and the ground for a bed represented true freedom. No worries, no responsibilities. But the sky rained and the ground was hard.

The more he drifted, the emptier he felt, like an unused toolshed.

He worked. He had money, but he worked because work gave him a sense of place. He hired out as a wrangler, a beginner's job. Keely was no beginner but it was work. The man who employed him was not a generous man. Cowboys by the dozens were looking for work because the winter storms had blown their previous jobs away. The rancher knew it and took advantage of their plight. He even cheated them on wages. When he tried that on Keely, Keely turned hard, gray eyes on the man's pinched face.

"You owe me ten more dollars," he said.

"That's for your board and bunk," the man said sharply.

"Bed and found come with any ranch job, and you know it," Keely told the rancher. Keely kept his calm, but he was seething.

"Not here, they don't, feller."

Keely grabbed his employer by the neck and shoulder and shook him until the man begged him to quit. The crew watched this performance with delight. They needed jobs and had given in to the rancher's greed, but each had wanted to do what Keely had just done.

"I want my ten!" Keely roared. "And I want it now!"

The rancher's face was purple, his eyes were glazed. Finally he reached into his pocket for a ten-dollar bill.

"Silver," Keely demanded.

"I ain't got it."

"Silver."

The man dug into his strongbox, then counted ten silver dollars into Keely's hand.

"You're fired!" the rancher screeched.

Keely rode off on Thorny while the men cheered. He rode toward the Rockies, which shimmered in the distance like a scaly dragon's tail. He had never been to the mountains and they were as good a destination as any other place. The emptiness inside grew as he put more space between himself and his home, the KM. He needed an anchor, and longed for three square meals a day and the same bed for a while. *You got to hang your hat someplace, fella,* he told himself. *Maybe a saddle bum can live from peak to valley, but not you.*

Halfway across the Rockies, in the middle of the Wind River Range, Keely was ambushed by three men with drawn pistols.

"No," he told them when they demanded his money. "You can't have it."

"Then we'll shoot you and take it, anyway," the leader of the trio threatened.

The leader was a red-faced, porky fellow, with a dark mustache that clashed with his crimson features. A high, peaked sombrero sat on top of his head.

"Where'd you get that silly hat?" Keely asked.

Thrown off guard for a second, the leader glanced up. His companions also glanced at the tent on his head, and one of them snickered. Keely drew his pistol and fired three times, hitting the weapon of each man. The weapons went spinning into the dirt. The men yelped like turpentined dogs.

"Hey!" yelled one, shaking his numbed hand. "You can't do that."

"I just did." Keely's gray eyes were even harder than they had been with the cheating rancher. "You three ride on!" he roared. "If I ever see any of you again, I'll shoot your noses off. Am I understood?"

There were no answers, so Keely shot the fallen pistols with three more blasts from his Colt. The guns were smashed. On the other hand, his own pistol was now empty.

The leader bared his teeth in an evil smile. "Now we got you," he said in triumph.

Keely pulled a bowie knife from its sheath on the back of his saddle. The blade was as sharp as a barber's razor and as broad as a woodsman's ax.

"No," he said, "you do not. If you come for me, I'll cut your noses off now. Maybe I won't stop at that."

He reloaded his pistol while the bandits watched in a sulky silence. Finished, he tipped his hat, a felt Stetson, and then headed Thorny toward the Snake River.

The Snake River country offered work at a sheep ranch. Being a cattleman, Keely didn't care much for sheep. Their sharp hooves could trample grass and ruin good range, but he worked there because he was curious about sheep.

"Do you think you'll make money at this?" he asked the owner.

"Sure," was the confident reply. "Wool brings a good price and mutton is always in demand."

Mutton? The cattleman in Keely felt his stomach dip. "But you don't have a railhead near," he said. "And you don't drive sheep like cattle."

"Wrong. You can drive sheep just like cattle, only they're a bit slower, being sheep. Why, they tell of a drover who took sheep clear from St. Louie to Canada, so I can probably get these to the Union Pacific easily."

Keely didn't hang around to see. He had learned as much about sheep as he wanted to know, and he didn't care for the smell, and so he left. Restless, he crossed over into Oregon and headed up the John Day country.

He came to a town called Placer and decided to stop overnight. He wanted a bath and a shave with hot water, and a good meal. Thorny needed rest and a good meal of oats. As soon as Thorny was properly housed, Keely found a hotel and checked in. He took his bath and had his shave, then went looking for a place to eat. Visions of a huge steak and fried potatoes topped off with a great slab of pie made his gut ache with anticipation.

Along the way he decided to have a drink, and he stopped off at the Gold Nugget Saloon. A Gold Nugget Saloon in a town called Placer hinted of mining, but Keely had seen nothing of mining operations. He'd seen sheep ranches and cattle ranches and even horse ranches, but nothing of mining. Probably mining had played out, as often happened. After mining, other activities moved in to keep the country going. The region looked strictly like ranching country to Keely.

He went into the Gold Nugget and ordered a whiskey. He downed it and asked for a beer.

"What's the matter?" a man at the bar asked. "Two whiskies too much for you, cowpoke?"

The man was tall and thin, with a hawk's sharp face and cruel eyes. He was smiling with bloodless lips.

"We don't think much of weaklings what drink just one slug and then that there beer. They's mama's boys what do that and we don't like them here."

The man was leaning his tall, thin body against the bar, his booted feet angling out. A bottle and a full shot glass rested on the bar in front of him. The bottle was half empty.

"Speak up, feller," the thin man commanded. "What's your excuse?"

Keely sighed. Trouble was staring him straight in the eye. It seemed that he was having more than his share lately.

Chapter Two

Keely didn't want trouble. He wasn't looking for it and he didn't want it to look for him. He turned his back on the belligerent talk from the skinny man.

"Hey, you! Don't turn your back on me, feller. I don't like it."

Keely wanted to tell him to go stick his head in a barrel, but he didn't. He kept his back turned. There were a lot of men in the bar. Several of them, Keely noted, were as skinny as the one who was badgering him. They looked alike and Keely judged that they were related. Brothers, maybe. Mean. Mean faces.

"He don't want none of you, Jeeter," said one of the thin men, a shadow under the flickering lamp. "You best go tease a dog."

19

"I want this son of a sissy dog right here," came the shrill response. "Turn around, dog."

This brought a raspy laugh from the onlookers. The thin men jiggled like underwear on a wash line.

Keely turned. He walked over to the man called Jeeter and reached up. He took the man's longish ear between his fingers and, with an iron grip, twisted it.

Jeeter let out a whoop.

"On your knees, you walking scrap pile," Keely ordered.

His captive's arms flailed the air like he was swatting mosquitoes. He screeched, "You'll break my ear, dang you! Leggo! Leggo!"

"On your knees before I yank this dried apricot clear off."

But Jeeter wasn't having any. His hand plunged for a pistol, low on his thigh. Keely cut down with his free hand, and Jeeter whooped again as his weapon went flying. Then Keely let him have it. He hit Jeeter with a blow that could be heard back in Gunny. The fellow's interest was abruptly transferred to the plank floor, which he hit very hard with his entire body. He lay still and stared slack-jawed at the ceiling.

Keely saw movement from the other skinny men, and he readied himself for more action, whether with fists or guns.

"Don't, gentlemen," he urged. "Let us part in peace."

Hands were stilled, undecided.

One of the skinnies stepped forward. He was taller and older than the others. He had the same hawk face as Jeeter, the same cruel eyes, but there was also the cunning of a fox in the thin face.

"What's your name?" he demanded. His tone was that of a man accustomed to getting quick and satisfactory answers.

"None of your business," Keely said.

The tall man flushed. "Well, listen up, cowboy. I'm Ivor Clatchett and that man on the floor is my brother. I don't like what you did to him."

"Well, well," Keely said.

The other skinny men gathered around Ivor Clatchett. They were joined by a man who was just as tall but smooth-skinned and heavy. Whereas the others were unkempt, he was well dressed, with his black hair slicked back and parted in the middle.

"We'll have to take you to jail," the smooth-skinned man said. "You're causing a disturbance."

"And who are you?" Keely asked.

"I'm Lyle Bolding, lawyer for the Clatchetts."

"That's fine. Now I want to tell you something, Lawyer Bolding." Keely nodded in the direction of the Clatchetts. "I started nothing. There are a score of witnesses who will testify to that." As shadows vanished through the batwing doors, Keely caught on to the situation. "Well, anyway, don't any of you scarecrows come near me or I'll knock you clear to Texas. That includes you, Tubby." He glared at Bolding.

And then he walked out into the clear night air. Though not followed, he heard Ivor Clatchett say, "Later, boys. Later. Let's take care of poor Jeeter first."

Keely went to the hotel for his saddlebags and then to the stable for Thorny. Thorny was a little grumpy about the interruption of a decent feed, but the two left the town of Placer without further trouble. Keely knew that he would probably have been shot in his sleep had he stayed at the hotel. If not that, then poor Thorny would have been hamstrung. Something like that would surely happen, and he didn't intend to find out just what.

The stars and moon were like street lamps in the sky. Keely easily found a trail and followed it. He didn't take the main road, for vengeance took the easy routes. It didn't matter where he went, and this trail was as good as any other.

After about an hour he came to a ranch tucked in the curve of a silvery river. Orange light softened the ground under the windows of what Keely took to be the family home. He caught the scent of roast beef and remembered that he hadn't eaten since morning. Thorny had enjoyed at least a partial helping of oats, but he'd had nothing at all.

The beef scent grew stronger and more enticing. Keely had eaten nothing but mutton at the sheep rancher's spread, and beef smelled like home to him. There was something about the scene that appealed to him. It was homey and comfortable, like one of those Christmas greeting cards but without snow. He made a sudden decision. This ranch, this cozy nook where the cooking smelled just fine and the orange lamplight beckoned like soft blankets, was going to be his home. This was what he'd been looking for. He was a long way from shortgrass country but he had suddenly found home again. If necessary, he'd work for nothing. No rancher could argue about those wages. He'd work for bed and board, and this place would become home. He could think here, come to grips with himself, and maybe his life would take a purposeful direction again.

He nudged Thorny across the clearing, dismounted, tied the reins to a rail, and knocked on the door. He sniffed. Man, did that beef smell good! His mouth watered. Surely he'd be invited in. Nobody ever turned down a stranger in these parts where hospitality was worn like a comfortable old shirt.

He knocked again. This time the door was flung open with a crash. A grim-faced man with a rifle met him. The muzzle was pointed straight at Keely's heart.

"Whoa!" Keely sputtered, taken by surprise. His homey dream had smashed into reality.

The man nodded. "Whoa right there!" he roared.

He was a big man, with a brown, weathered face. He gripped the rifle firmly, ready for whatever might come. Beyond him, at the table, Keely saw a woman and two young children. A girl in her late teens sat next to the woman.

"I don't mean any harm," Keely said quickly. "I just smelled roast beef, and thought . . . well. . . ."

"You can tell Ivor Clatchett that his tricks won't work," the man said, totally ignoring Keely's amiable tone. "You're working for him, right? You're supposed to make me an offer for my place! Spy on me!"

"No," Keely said in the most sincere voice he could muster. "You're wrong. I've met Ivor Clatchett and his clan and I hate them." He held up his fist. The knuckles were skinned where they had landed on Jeeter's bony jaw. "One of those people owes me some skin. I lent it to him fresh tonight."

The other man stared, not quite believing. Keely reached over and gently turned the rifle aside. "You don't want to pull that trigger, really. But if you thought I was a Clatchett man, I wouldn't blame you."

"Cy, ask him in for coffee," the mistress of the house suggested.

"I don't know, Mary." Cy's voice was faltering. "I don't know."

"I just came into the country," Keely said. "I don't even know you. I just smelled your fine cooking."

The rifle went down. "No," the rancher said, "I wasn't going to shoot you. I have never shot a man in my life, but I might shoot a Clatchett. Oh, yes." His voice turned bitter. "I might shoot a Clatchett." He leaned his rifle next to the door. "Come in."

Keely entered, removing his Stetson. As he stood uncertainly, Mary beckoned to him. "Come, Mr. . . . ? Have coffee with us."

"My name is McGuire, ma'am, Keely McGuire, and if you don't mind, I'd as soon have beef along with that coffee."

The younger children giggled and the girl smiled. Keely liked her at once. Her wide-set eyes examined him frankly. She was pretty, with auburn hair tumbling over her shoulders like a waterfall spray.

"I'll set you a place," she offered, and Keely liked her voice too. In a harsh frontier setting, he listened for the harsher sounds in life, but the girl's voice was soft and melodious.

Chairs were scraped aside and another one was slipped in. A plate appeared, loaded with roast beef, mashed potatoes and gravy, and peas. *The family might be frightened by the Clatchetts,* Keely thought, *but that doesn't stunt their generosity.*

"My name is Mossman," his host said when everybody was settled again. "Cy Mossman, and Mary is my wife." His voice struck a note of pride. "She's so pretty and young looking that people mistake her for my daughter."

Mary blushed. "Cy, stop that. You're embarrassing me—and probably Mr. McGuire."

"And my older girl," Mossman went on, smiling, "the one who seems to have taken a shine to you, is Margaret. We call her Marcy. The boy is Robert and my younger daughter is Jacqueline—Jackie. And," he added with pride, "they're all good hands.

Robert can handle a span of four Appa-loosas already."

Keely responded while he shoveled in potatoes, "I'm glad to meet all of you."

"And you, Mr. McGuire," Marcy asked politely, "are you traveling through?"

"Can't say," Keely replied with a touch of mystery. And then, knowing that some history was wanted, he added, "I had a ranch in Wyoming."

"Oh?" The girl was curious. "What happened?"

"What kind of a winter did you have here?" Keely asked.

"Not bad," Mossman said. "It gets cold, but the weather was no worse or better than usual."

"Ever hear about the blizzards east of the Rockies?"

"Sure have." Mossman's eyes narrowed. "Were you caught in them?"

"Along with a hundred others in my part of the country. I was wiped out."

As he progressed with his meal, coming in for seconds, Keely related the events of the past terrible year. It was the first time he'd spoken about it in detail to anybody since leaving the KM. As he talked, he began to feel better and lighter, as if a load was lifting from his spirit.

"It wasn't a good time," he finished, helping himself to a piece of apple pie. "And now that I've bored you with my tale, may I ask, Mr. Mossman, what do you have here—sheep?"

"Yes, I have sheep, but also cattle and horses, Appaloosas. I'm experimenting. What does best, I'll specialize in later."

"What do you think it will be?"

"Well," Mossman said thoughtfully, "I know you're a cattleman, being from Plains Country, but sheep look pretty good here. Cattle are still doing fine—there are big yards in Pendleton—but I think sheep will take over."

Keely nodded. He understood. A man had to do what was necessary to survive. If sheep were it, then sheep it was.

"I'd like to work for you," he said.

Mossman looked at him in surprise. "A cattleman working on a mostly sheep ranch?"

"I've worked with them." Keely told of his experience with his last employer. "Besides," he finished with a grin, "you still have cattle and horses."

"But I'm not in the market for a man. Marcy helps on the range and the kids help in the yard. I can't afford a man." He glanced at his wife. "Mary's the book-keeper and she says no hired help for a while."

It was then that Keely sprang his deal: "I'll work for nothing, just bed and board."

Mossman's eyes widened. "Why? There are ranchers around here who could pay you."

"I like your roast beef."

Glancing at his wife, Mossman caught some kind of signal. "Listen," he said, "there's an extra room in the barn. We'll sleep on this and talk in the morning."

Keely nodded. Fair enough. Any sensible rancher would view such an offer carefully. What lay behind it? Was the man who called himself Keely McGuire really a Clatchett spy? A family discussion was in order.

The next morning Mossman came to the point at once: "You're hired under your suggested conditions. No pay, but board and room. Maybe after the roundup this fall, I can give you some back wages if all goes well. But," he added, and his eyes narrowed, "if I even suspect you are a Clatchett man, you are gone. Is it a deal?"

"A deal."

The men shook hands and Keely went to work. He was more contented than he had been for a long time. He had known a man once who said, "Contentment makes a man soft." The man was a hard man. He smoked cigars halfway down and chewed the rest. He was a cattle buyer from Chicago and he wasn't soft. But he died of a heart attack at the age of thirty-five. Keely didn't know what to make of that, but he knew one thing: He would take a chance on contentment. If it made a man soft, let it.

The Mossman ranch wasn't the largest in the region. The China Ranch in the John Day country made the Mossman holdings seem puny, but Mossman didn't have to step down to anybody. His ranch was, he said, "Big enough to keep beans on the table—and even good beef now and then." But it was, Keely learned, much larger than that. Mossman was being polite, or cautious—Keely wasn't sure which. The

Clatchett name was brought up more than once. Obviously, they were much on Mossman's mind.

"That Bolding fellow offered me three thousand for this place," he said indignantly one day. "Heck, this here ground is worth ten—no, twenty—times that."

"Clatchetts seem to be important around here," Keely said.

"They certainly think they are. They came into this country about five years ago and now own about all of it, I guess. They want my place too." Mossman scowled. "The only way they'll get it will be over my dead body."

Life at the ranch wasn't all work. Sundays were for resting after a few early chores. Sundays were a time for picnics and walks in the countryside. The two children didn't go to a regular school. The nearest was far away in Placer, and so they studied at home under the guidance of their mother. On Sundays they read aloud from their *McGuffey's Reader* for family entertainment. Marcy read Shakespeare and poetry in a voice that warmed Keely's heart. She was an accomplished banjo player, and Keely joined the family in song and enjoyed himself immensely. It was great to be part of such a close group where love was not spoken about but expressed in deed.

However, it was the picnics that Keely enjoyed most. On these occasions he found he could be closer to Marcy. The favorite picnic ground was a grove about a mile from the ranch. They always walked there, and Keely made it a point to walk at Marcy's side. They talked. It was mostly small talk about the weather, the ranch, and family life, but sometimes Marcy would mention the Clatchetts.

"I hate them," she said one day in a voice very unlike her usual civilized tones. "They are evil men and will harm us someday. I'm sure of it."

Not, Keely vowed to himself, *as long as I'm here.*

Divining the look on his face, Marcy said, "I'm so glad you're here. Father stands up for his rights and won't be walked on, but— Well, two brave men are better than one."

Keely wanted to take the girl in his arms and comfort her. He didn't do so, of course, but the feeling was so strong between them that Marcy moved closer to his side as they walked, and the harmony between them was like honey to Keely.

As the summer went by, the feeling for Marcy grew in Keely, and he was sure that Marcy returned his feelings. One day while they were alone in the grove, Keely dared to speak something of his thoughts.

"You know I'm fond of you, Marcy," he said gently. "I guess it shows. I wonder if your father minds."

"Probably," was the shy response. "But give him time. Let him know you better."

There was a promise in her voice that gave Keely's heart a flip. He wasn't new to romance at twenty-nine, but he had never felt toward any other woman as he did toward Marcy. He hardly knew the girl, yet he was—what? In love? How did a man know when he was in love! The only comparison he had to fall back on was that his previous ventures into a woman's companionship had never resulted in the same feelings he had for Marcy. He thought about her constantly, loved her presence, her voice, her goodness, her refinement.

Keely realized that, as Marcy had

pointed out, it was necessary to gain Mossman's confidence. He carried out with efficiency his duties, which ranged from stableboy to veterinarian. Though he was not so good with sheep, he was an expert when it came to horses and cattle. He knew how to handle them better than Mossman, who eventually turned those animals over to him.

"We've been here five years," Mossman remarked one evening, "and I've had a dozen hired hands when I could afford them, but you know more than all of them put together." He scratched his head. "I still don't know why you're working for nothing, but I'm sure glad you're around."

Mossman's statement suggested to Keely that his boss was putting more and more trust in him. That, in turn, opened a door, and he spoke to Marcy about marriage the following Sunday.

She responded by kissing him. It was a sweet kiss, and her lips lingered before she drew back. Then she laid her head on his chest and murmured, "There is your answer, my dear love." She hesitated a few moments, then added, "Father likes you. Still, I think you ought to wait."

"For how long?" Keely hoped that his impatience was understandable to her.

"Till after the fall roundup. Work with him until then. He likes you, but trust doesn't come easily for him. The Clatchetts have turned him into a suspicious man."

So Keely had to endure love's waiting game. In the meantime his eyes and heart feasted on Marcy. He marveled. In addition to her other accomplishments she painted landscapes in oils. During Sunday readings, her voice, both womanly and alluring, roved over passages of poetry like a prairie breeze. She was always neat, even after a long day over washtubs or at baking. Her auburn hair glistened in both lamplight and sun, and the sight always took Keely's breath away.

He realized that he was very much in love. His world was here, centered around a girl with the lovely name of Marcy Mossman, and he waited impatiently for fall to come so that he could ask Mossman for her hand.

Chapter Three

Keely was working in the barn when the Clatchetts paid their first visit to the ranch. He saw them through the door, five skinny figures astride five fat horses. Lyle Bolding was with them, his bare head shining like a black melon.

Cy Mossman met them angrily. He stood erect and still, a rigid symbol of belligerence.

"Get off my property," he ordered.

"Now, Mr. Mossman," Ivor Clatchett said smoothly, "all we want to do is talk."

"You want to steal my ranch like you done a dozen others," was the blunt response. "Well, it won't work. I ask you to leave. My place isn't for stealing."

Bolding spoke up: "Are you so sure you own this property, Mossman?"

37

"What's that supposed to mean?"

"I mean there are a lot of ranches here-
abouts, and they are big. Very big. They
don't know quite where their boundaries
are. We think you are squatting on some
of their ground."

"What's that supposed to mean?" Mossman repeated, his voice husky with tension and anger.

"It means this—if you don't own all
your ground or a large part of it, you can
lose it, and we intend to investigate that.
Now, we can save everybody trouble.
We'll give you three—no," he continued
with a smile, "five thousand dollars for
your ranch. You can walk off with five
thousand clear."

"But tell me this," Mossman challenged.
"If the ground does't belong to me, as you
think, why would it belong to you if *you*
bought it?"

"We have the money and lawyer talent
to fight this possible illegality of yours in
the courts. We can win."

"Bolding," Mossman said in a voice that
put an end to the discussion, "you are an
outright crook. Your whole story is a lie

and you know it. My land is free and clear. Now get off, all of you!"

There followed a silence as grim as the smile of a skull. The Clatchetts were grouped together, a spindly scarecrow knot of humanity, all scowling. Some rested their hands on the butts of their holstered pistols. Finally Keely stepped into view and took up a position beside his employer.

"That's him!" Jeeter yelped. "That's the bum what busted my jaw."

His jaw was wrapped in bandages and his voice came out muffled, as if he were yelping from the bottom of a well.

"My pleasure," Keely said with a smile. "Anybody else want one? I give them free."

"Don't get smart, mister," Ivor warned, his hawk's eyes bleak.

"Mr. Mossman ordered you off his property," Keely went on, ignoring Ivor's advice. "So I think your talk is over. *Git!*"

Jeeter went for his gun, but stopped, paralyzed when he saw Keely's big-barreled Colt .44.

"Don't do it!" Keely roared. "Now all of you leave!"

Ivor Clatchett's face was tight with rage. "We'll come back," he snarled. "And when we do, feller, you had better not be here."

"My name is Keely McGuire, not 'feller.'"

Ivor glared, then turned his horse and galloped off, followed by the rest. They rode straight out and didn't look back, but Keely knew by the hunch of their shoulders that they were furious.

"You didn't have to do that," Mossman said. "This isn't your fight."

"Oh, I think it is. I work for you, and that makes me part of it."

"That the way they do it where you came from?"

"Yes."

"They mean trouble. Bad trouble. Lot of ranchers have been leaving lately, and the Clatchetts always end up with their ground." Mossman shook his head. "Don't tell the others they were here."

It happened that Mrs. Mossman and Marcy were in back of the house doing the laundry. The big tubs of water were being heated over open fires, which was cooler for them in summer. The children were up the river gathering dried bark, one of their chores. The bark from fallen trees was used in starting fires, and it made an excellent, tinderlike kindling. Sacks of it were stored in the barn.

Keely agreed that it would serve no purpose to speak of the incident, but when he and Marcy went for a walk that evening, he had never felt more protective in his life. He slipped an arm around her waist, a bold act, but it seemed so natural that he wasn't in the least apologetic. They stopped and he kissed her. She responded with fire and Keely hugged her to him. What a gracious and wonderful woman she was. How had he been so lucky? From an aimless wanderer to a man in love was a long step, the step of giants. But he was an ordinary mortal. How did it happen?

"I never knew I could fall in love," he whispered.

"But you did?"

"You know I did."

"With whom, Mr. McGuire?" she asked. She was smiling, teasing.

"You know who I love."

"Well, I declare, what a coincidence."

"Oh?"

"Yes. It just happens that I'm in love with you."

They kissed again, and held each other, and Keely felt her heart beating. But into that moment of extreme happiness there fell a shadow. For some unexplained reason, Keely felt loneliness. Loneliness? Love was supposed to bring joy, and he was happy, but there at the edges, like a bird of prey about to dive, was an unmistakable loneliness. As he hugged Marcy to him, he was happy and, at the same time, afraid. Even he knew that love should never be lonely.

He asked Marcy about it, and she shook her head, puzzled. "Why would you feel lonely? I don't. I feel warm inside. I feel like my world is complete, because I have met the most wonderful man ever. That's what love is, isn't it? Isn't love happiness?"

"Yes," Keely agreed, and he chased the great bird of loneliness from his thoughts. Love was happiness.

In spite of his victory, however, he lost the fight. Loneliness persisted. He continued to fight gallantly, but he had met a determined enemy. Because of his mixed feelings, he loved Marcy more, and he was tender with her, and held her to his breast so that he could feel her strong heart beating, assuring him that all was well.

The second time the Clatchett gang came, a week later, Keely was not at the ranch. He was mending fence a mile away. His mind was on Marcy and what they would do after they married. He was quite certain by now that her father would approve. Mossman's confidence in and appreciation of him went up by the day.

Keely wondered if he should try Wyoming again. He liked Oregon, but he did, after all, still own the KM. In spite of the brutality of the past winter, Keely discovered anew that he felt a kinship with the land. He also preferred working for himself. Though there were a hundred more headaches in being self-employed, he was answerable to only to one taskmaster— himself. He'd been lucky. The KM spread had come into his hands cheaply through a bankruptcy sale, the previous owner having failed due to weather too. He had started small, but in five years had been able to buy more land and more cattle.

With a wife like Marcy, a man could return, start over again, and succeed.

The thought of the girl made him smile. She was never far from his mind. He might be roping a calf and, for some danged reason, the girl's face would pop into his mind. No connection at all between the bawling calf and Marcy, but there it was. He might be splicing wire as he was now, and there was Marcy, gracing his mind with her lovely eyes and sweet face. The thought of her gave him the shivers, and he delighted in them. No other woman had even given Keely McGuire the shivers though a few had tried.

Old-timers called barbed wire "the devil's hatband." They hated it because it foreshadowed the closing of open range. Cattlemen fought its coming, sometimes to the death, but it came anyhow, as relentlessly as the flow of farmers who accompanied it. Keely could take fencing or leave it. Fencing had become fairly common by the time he bought the KM, and he had both closed and open range. Fences were handy because, preventing cattle from grazing onto neighboring ranges, they saved roundup time. Farmers used it to keep cattle from chewing up their crops.

Keely was thinking about those things and of Marcy, as always, when the first shots sounded. He didn't think much about them. Cy Mossman often banged away at chicken-stealing coyotes. Foxes were also a problem, and Mossman had a lot of their hides nailed to his barn.

But as the shots persisted, turning into a queer and ominous thunder, Keely leaped upon Thorny and raced toward the ranch. He knew instinctively what to expect— there was a battle going on between Mossman and the Clatchetts. A big battle. By the sound of the guns, both Marcy and Mrs. Mossman were involved. They could shoot because Cy had taught them.

As Keely dashed like a spear through the vacant fields that made up much of the ranch, his heart chilled. The shooting had stopped, and the sudden silence was the most fearful sign of all that something awful awaited him. He reached the clearing to confront a scene of horror. The two women, Marcy and her mother, lay on the ground side by side. Cy lay near them. Judging by the position of his body, he had been crawling toward the women but died before reaching them. As Keely drew Thorny to a halt, there were screams from the house, followed by a series of shots. Then all was quiet, like the stillness after a storm.

Jeeter, Ivor, and Turk emerged from the house.

"Dang it!" Jeeter complained. "I don't like killing kids that way." He turned to Ivor. "That's the last time. Drown 'em, yes, but I don't like that shootin' and the way they look at you."

"Shut up," Ivor ordered. "We can't have witnesses, and you know it. You just do your job. You're good at it and that's why I have you do it."

Turk, a man with a knife scar on his left cheek, was grinning. The scar drew itself into a slit, sharp like the blade that had created it.

"See your brother there?" Ivor said. "He isn't complaining, so shut up and be a man like him."

Keely sat astride Thorny, transfixed, riveted to his saddle like a bronze statue in a village square. He was stunned, the breath knocked out of him by what he was seeing and hearing. The gang hadn't sighted him yet because he'd come up from behind and all eyes were on the house.

"We get 'em all?" Bolding inquired anxiously.

"Except that saddle bum," Ivor replied.

"We got to get him."

"All we have to do is wait. He'll be along."

It was then that Keely snapped out of his shock. He drew his pistol and rode straight into the Clatchetts, firing as he charged.

"It's him!" Bolding cried. "Get him! Quick!"

But there was no getting Keely McGuire. He rode screaming like an unearthly horseman, a devil's spirit. He drove straight into the gang, scattering them in all directions.

The Clatchetts and Bolding returned his fire, but he spun Thorny around and around, and the others dared not fire too much lest they hit one of their own.

In a brief but horrifying moment he would never forget, Keely saw Marcy's body up close. He saw the others too, but he saw Marcy most clearly. She had been shot between her wide, lovely eyes, which now stared sightlessly at the sky. Her auburn hair was bloody and her breast was bloody too, for she had been shot several times. All of the Mossmans had been shot more than once, and there were no firearms belonging to the Mossmans in sight. They had been unarmed. The gang had slaughtered them, and because of the number of shots fired, the gang had taken their time.

Keely drove Thorny straight at Ivor Clatchett, shooting away at the murderer. He crashed into the man's horse and threw him to the ground. In the next moment Keely was thrown from Thorny. There were more shots from the gang, but luck held for Keely. It was still too dangerous for shots to be fired indiscriminately for fear of hitting one another. Keely flipped back on Thorny, fired again, and heard the hammer click on an empty cylinder. In a moment of clarity he realized that he didn't have a chance. The gang wanted him dead, because live men tell tales to sheriffs. If he continued to fight his one-sided battle, he would die. He put the spurs to Thorny, and the horse plunged out of the circle of men.

"After him!" Bolding ordered. "We got to get him."

The four youngest Clatchetts put their mounts into action. As Keely sped past the main house he cried out, "If I live, kids, I'll get even for you. I swear it!"

The part of the ranch that lay before him now was deeply forested. It was part of the great woodland that stretched to the Northwest, stopping only at the sea. The trees were thick and he passed from sight almost at once. The Clatchetts, however, were close behind. They were so close that one shot grazed Keely's side and he bled. It was not a serious wound, and he kept going though warm blood saturated his trouser leg. Thorny's hooves pounded like pistons in a steam engine.

As he reloaded and shot back, Keely fired blindly, shooting to intimidate as much as to hit. But his pursuers clung to his trail grimly. Their job was to kill a witness to a heinous crime, and they meant to do it. When Keely caught a glimpse of the outlaw posse, he fired at once. Twice he heard yelps, but all four continued to chase at top speed. Their wounds could not have been serious. The enemy flicked in and out of sight, reds, browns, yellows, blinking like dots and dashes in some kind of code among the greenery of the forest.

Thorny was tough. He had been driven many miles from his Wyoming home. He wasn't rusty in the joints, even though he had lazed at Mossman's considerably. Keely used the rancher's horses for work, but this happened to be a day when he had decided Thorny needed a change from the corral. He thanked heaven for that. There wasn't a horse in the West with more endurance than his faithful Thorny.

Keely heard the Clatchetts in the distance.

"I think he's gone that way."

"No, he ain't, you dog head. He cut up that there draw."

Keely crouched low, making as small a target as possible, but he realized that the men after him wouldn't hesitate to gun Thorny down too. This was not a Queen's Rules shooting match they were playing. Everything was a fair target, including Thorny. The horse was carrying a witness to a crime of the century and he would be shot, if possible. The horse, once downed, would leave their man afoot and easier to find and kill.

Guns continued to blast. Most of the shots were random, but some came close. Keely heard branches crackle as hot lead whipped through.

The pursuit lasted for the rest of the day. It lasted until horses and men on both sides were exhausted. Even Thorny was lathered, his withers gleaming with sweat. Still, Keely didn't dare ease up, and he urged the horse on. Thorny worked his heart out, doing his best for a master who had always been good to him.

Finally, night tossed a blanket over earth and the chase halted. Keely listened, his ears straining like water through tight silk, and he heard the Clatchetts about a hundred yards away. They were holding council.

"I think we lost 'im."

"Naw, we ain't. He's no ghost."

"Not yet." .

A guffaw.

Keely listened with a heart full of anguish and hate. He checked his pistol. Should he charge back and kill as many as he could? What sweet revenge that would be. What a relief from his grief. He wanted to avenge Marcy. He wanted to avenge the children and the older Mossmans. His whole being yearned and commanded him to smash and shoot and kill.

He drew his weapon and remained astride Thorny, deciding what to do.

"I reckon we just got to wait till tomorrow," Jeeter said in disgust. "Can't see my nose in front of my face. He could be waiting to pick us off in this here dark."

"We ought to push on," Turk advised. "He could sneak away."

"If we catch 'im, what'll we do?"

The voice was new to Keely.

"Sag, you're a snake-brain," Jeeter hissed. "What do you think—make him hotcakes? Kill 'im dead, man. *Dead!*"

"We oughter git back and bury them people too," came another voice, also new to Keely.

"I guess, Morey, that brother Ivor and Bolding can do some work." Jeeter's voice was triumphant. "Let 'em dig."

The others chuckled.

"Say," came the thin voice of Turk, "did you see that older girl? She really flew in

Ivor afore he got her between those pretty eyes."

It was then that Keely was tested to the quick. His finger rested on the trigger of his Colt .44. He could get one, maybe two, before they got him. He aimed his weapon at a silhouette. His finger tightened around the trigger. One squeeze and a Clatchett would soil the depths of hell. One squeeze, that was all. But Keely's finger rested just before the mechanism releasing the hammer let go. It wouldn't do. He wanted them all, especially Ivor and Bolding. To risk getting killed for only a part of his reward was not enough. If he didn't live, the brains of a cruel, ruthless gang would survive. Keely didn't want that. There was in him now an anguish so deep that only death could relieve it. And it must not be his own death.

He shoved his gun back into its holster and dismounted carefully. Careful not to make sounds, such as whipping a branch or stepping on one, he led Thorny off. He had no idea where he was going, because he didn't know the country. All he knew was that he would need to be a long way off for a while. The dead face of Marcy lay

in his mind like a nightmare. He saw again
her sightless eyes, her lovely hair matted
with blood, her graceful figure, and it was
then that he realized why he'd felt the
strangle of loneliness while she was alive.
He had known in some way that tragedy
lay ahead. Given Cy Mossman's fear of
the gang, it was not difficult, in retrospect,
to figure out what could happen. But he
had ignored the signs, not knowing exactly
what they meant. He would curse himself
for that for a long time to come. A long
time.

At intervals, as he traveled, Keely
asked himself if he was having a nightmare. Would he soon wake up and find
he'd experienced a horrible dream? But
when his wounded side began to sting, he
knew that he was not experiencing a nightmare in his sleep. He was living one.

In the days that followed he saw no
more Clatchetts. He had given them the
slip successfully. He made plans. He
would return to Placer and kill the Clatchetts. He would do it by stealth, taking
them one at a time from ambush. He felt
no guilt about this. The gang was com-
prised of bushwhackers, men who killed

from hiding or who slaughtered unarmed people without mercy. They themselves deserved no better treatment. If necessary, he would stand toe to toe and fight it out with one and all, but one way or another they would all die.

At first he was impatient to return to Placer and get the job done, but he decided against that. He was sure that the Mossman deaths would be blamed on him. Ivor would do that. Keely McGuire was only a drifter, as far as the community was concerned. He was a saddle bum, a scamp. Ivor would claim that he'd come upon the massacre and scared the criminal off, but he had escaped. The motive was robbery—Ivor had just paid five thousand in gold for the Mossman ranch. There would be a reward offered and every able-bodied man in the country would be looking for the vicious killer of the Mossmans.

No, it wouldn't do to return. Not yet. He would return—but not now. There would be a proper time for it. Let the excitement die down. Let the Clatchetts relax their guard. As arrogant as they were, they'd never suspect vengeance from a saddle bum. Yes, he would return, but at the proper time for surprise. Surprise would be his best ally.

Keely quit shaving. He did not wash. He hardly ate. Thorny got his feed, but he himself ate little. He couldn't eat. He couldn't believe the horror of his life but he knew it was true, and no food tempted him. He lost all desire to be clean and he grew as dirty as garbage. His beard was thick, red, and snarled, and he didn't care. A useful side effect to this new appearance was that the beard served as a disguise, but that was incidental. Uppermost in his mind was the killing of Clatchetts. He would get the entire gang. There was no other reason left for him to live.

Chapter Four

K eely pushed a weary Thorny north and west. He traveled many weeks before his mind began to function properly. A plan formed. Before, his thoughts had been skewered with splintery flashes of revenge in many ways, but he was now able to form a solid plan. But first he needed a place to stay, an anchor.

After a month of zigzagging across country, he met a man dressed in the skins of wolves and mountain lions. He was mounted on a mule and led a packhorse. They met on a remote trail in the upper Idaho country.

"Why don't you ride the horse and use the mule for packing?" Keely asked.

He could speak now. There had been weeks when he refused to talk, the very words seeming too much a burden to bother with. If he stopped in a town for supplies, he jabbed a finger at items he wanted. He muttered "oats" for Thorny. That was it, but now he was loosening up. The hate and grief had crystallized in him, and he could talk around it. He couldn't talk his hate away or defuse it in words. Like his soul, hate had become a part of him and it drove him. He lived on his hate and, learning to live with it, he could indulge in the trivialities of everyday life again, which included talk.

"Because I like it this way," the man in skins told him. "Any of your business?"

"Nope. Just seemed natural."

"What's natural for some is unnatural for others."

"True," Keely agreed, thinking of his mission. It would be as natural for him to kill Clatchetts as for others to stamp out rats. "Where am I?" he asked.

"Dumb question."

"I ask dumb questions."

The man in skins looked at Keely for several studied moments. The man had keen eyes. He had seen much in the wilderness, and he had had years of lone living in which he'd speculated about the nature of man, and he knew men well in spite of his isolation.

He said to Keely, "You are in trouble if you don't know where you are."

"Could be."

"You are in north Idyho. You got other troubles too, eh?"

"Could be," Keely repeated.

"Where are you heading?"

"I don't care. Where are *you* going?"

"Port Townsend up on the Strait of Juan de Fuca." He pointed at his loaded packhorse. "Got furs to trade."

"Mind if Thorny and I tag along?"

"Yes, I do mind."

"You don't like people much, do you?"

"Not if they's all like me, and I judge they are."

"Well, how's about Thorny and me following about, say, half a mile behind. We won't be with you then."

The man in skins grinned. "You still got your sense of humor."

"Then we can come along?"

"If you don't talk too much."

"I won't say a word. Neither will my horse."

"He can talk. Horses often say something worth hearing."

Keely stuck out his hand. "My name is McGuire. What's yours?"

"They call me Skins."

"Can't see why."

Skins snorted and started his mule along the trail. Before they'd gone far he said, "Son, I don't know who you are after, but I'll tell you something—I wouldn't want to be them. No, sir. I'd take a pack of wolves anytime."

Keely didn't respond, and the two continued in silence. In fact, little was said for the rest of the journey, though Skins seemed to enjoy the company.

They reached Townsend in a week, and Keely didn't like the place. The town was mad with shipping. Oceangoing vessels dotted the roadsteads, and the docks were full. The ships brought cargo from far places and sailed off with lumber and logs, the principal exports. Sailors crowded the streets, along with landsmen. Businessmen were everywhere, identified by their tall hats and gold watch chains. Shopkeepers and bartenders thrived. It was the most congested and disorderly city Keely had seen since a visit to St. Louis in his youth.

"What's happening here?" he asked Skins before they parted.

"Townsend's going to be the capital of this whole Northwest, is what," Skins claimed with surprising pride. "Even going to beat Astoria and Portland. Yes sir. They's a railroad coming here, and when it does, well, old Townsend will be another Chicago, I can tell you."

Keely wasn't impressed by progress. He stayed the night and pushed on. He didn't want crowds. He had regained his composure, but he would never care for the hassle of civilization. He went up the coast, driving Thorny easy. He went to Blyn, then Dungeness, both ports on the Strait. He didn't like them, either, though neither was as wild as Townsend.

He headed north and west again, following the coast, and came to the town of Port Angeles, Port of the Angels. It was a moderate-sized town, with dirt streets, boardwalks, and the inevitable shipping. Keely would have continued on up-coast, where there were smaller settlements, but he was tired. Besides, he figured he was far enough from the Clatchett gang by now. He found a vacant cabin on the shore, about a mile from Angeles, and settled down. It was here that he would perfect his plan before returning to Placer.

In spite of its beauty, Keely didn't care for the country much. The Olympic Mountains were too tall for him, too formidable, a scowling backdrop. He preferred the Plains Country, where a man could see in all directions clear to the horizon. This country was swathed in timber, which was creating a boom and drawing big money all along the coast. Timber was the main attraction, and it was being harvested as fast as axes and crosscut saws could work. There were trees so huge that Keely whistled in amazement. But their main interest for him was their fortresslike possibilities. A man could tuck himself away forever in the woods and never be found.

He repaired the cabin, finding release in the work. Working kept his mind off Marcy's dead body. And while he worked a girl watched him. She was curious about this stranger. Many strangers arrived, but this one with the red beard, who kept to himself, seemed to intrigue her. She was of mixed race, her mother being a Dolamish Indian, her father a wandering trapper. She was called Tanada, a lovely sounding name that meant "graveyard" in English. She lived alone, wanted by neither her tribe nor the whites, and she survived. She could have told Keely how to fix his cabin without spending so much money. The roof could have been repaired with the bark of trees, for instance. But she maintained her distance and silence, and Keely did not know she was there.

Since Thorny needed some kind of shelter against the rains that swept like a wet broom back and forth across the rugged landscape, Keely built him a lean-to behind the cabin. It wasn't exactly an edifice of beauty, because Keely was a cattleman, not a builder. Thorny, for his part, had never been under shelter in his life, and when he hesitated to enter the structure, Keely told him, "Maybe it isn't much, you ungrateful plug, but it will keep the rain off your ungrateful head. Now git!" And Thorny got.

When he wasn't pounding nails, Keely put part one of his plan into action. He practiced with his pistol. Knowing a pistol would not be enough firepower for the action he had in mind, he bought a .44–40 Winchester lever-action rifle. The gun held fifteen rounds of ammunition and was of the same caliber as his pistol. Six and fifteen gave a total of twenty-one shots. Keely was satisfied. He might need them all.

For the next two days he practiced, and the skies billowed under pressuring echoes. The Angeles police paid him a visit.

"You can't shoot like that," one of them said.

"Why not?"

"Because you might hit somebody."

"I'm not aiming toward town, my friend."

"Well, we think it's against the law, all that racket. Makes people nervous."

"Sorry about making people nervous, but as far as the law is concerned you can't touch me. You are city police and this is country."

"I'll get Sheriff Williamson, then."

"Go ahead," Keely invited. "Get two of him."

"You better quit it," the officer advised.

His companions, two men with droopy black mustaches, glowered.

The three men left, and Keely continued to shoot. He went to town the next day and bought more ammunition. He expected to be stopped by the police, and he was. A short, muscular man stepped from a building with a false front. He had a ruddy, square-jawed face, and light blue eyes that had seen much of death and violence. He was followed by the same fellow who had questioned Keely about his shooting. "That's him, Sheriff," he said petulantly.

"I'm Williamson," the short man said. "You're making a lot of noise up at your place. Any reason?"

"Just having some fun, Sheriff."

The lawman nodded. "Can't see any harm in that, but I'll tell you something— keep it up and we'll blue-ticket you right out of the country."

Keely knew that they meant he'd be escorted out of the region and advised to keep going.

"That's not nice," he said.

"Didn't catch your name," Williamson said.

"Didn't give it."

"Give it." There was a steely insistence in the demand that Keely couldn't ignore, and he gave his name.

"I'm going to check you out. Where'd you say you came from?"

"I didn't say."

"Don't play games, mister."

"Over in Wyoming. I had a spread there, the KM. It's near Gunny. You can check it out."

"I will. Why did you leave?"

"Ever hear of last winter?" Keely found himself growing testy. The sheriff was a tough man. So was Keely McGuire.

Williamson studied Keely a minute, then nodded. "Yeah, I heard. That was bad, but sympathy aside, you keep on shooting and you're gone."

Keely nodded. He had lost the round. He wanted to keep his identity to himself, but Williamson was not to be fooled with. Williamson was going to check his story, and if the trail Williamson followed led to Placer and the Mossman ranch, Keely would be in big trouble. It was an unfortunate situation, and there was only one solution. He wasn't satisfied with his rifle shooting. He was not good enough yet to stand up to the Clatchett gang. Neither did he want a blue ticket, so the solution was to practice farther away, far enough so that Angeles law couldn't hear. When he felt he was good enough, he would return to Placer and give Angeles law its peace again. That time would not be long. He was getting better with the .44–40 every day.

Unknown to Keely, there were two more people interested in his shooting. One was Tanada. She watched the man with the red beard when he was practicing with his weapons. She knew why he was practicing. The man was expecting trouble. She had seen him use his pistol and he was good. He was not good with the rifle, but he wanted to be good and that meant he intended to use it. He didn't want to use it for hunting elk or deer. A person didn't have to be especially good to hit them. No, this man who practiced so steadily was after bigger targets—men. And they would be men who shot back.

Watching Keely practice, Tanada divined all of this. She didn't know any details, but she knew what the wilderness had taught her: No one wasted ammunition just shooting. It was too expensive. One shot, one deer. Many shots—trouble.

The second person interested in Keely's target practice was Josh Deerface, a Tlingit Indian, an escaped slave of the Dolamish tribe. When Keely went to town for ammunition the second time, Josh helped himself to Keely's food, then hid again. He would continue to watch the white man, because he was hungry. He existed on roots and berries, but he needed more, and was losing the battle of survival. He was as thin as grass and the white man had plenty of grub.

Keely moved his practicing area four or five miles up-coast. He wanted to return to Placer as soon as possible and settle the main event in his life—revenge for the slaughter of the Mossmans, especially of his beloved Marcy. He would not rest until the terrible people who had killed an innocent family were under the ground. He didn't want them brought to court. The justice of courts was slow, and smart lawyers could get killers off. The Clatchetts could afford smart lawyers. Keely wanted real justice, by hot lead. Only that would do, and he would die in the attempt to administer it, if necessary.

A couple of days after his second visit to town for ammunition, Keely again went to Angeles. Josh Deerface immediately helped himself to food. He didn't care much for the white man's vittles, preferring dried salmon and seal meat, but it did fill the stomach and was easy to get.

Keely approached Angeles with unaccustomed tension. He lived with the philosophy that what was going to be was going to be, and he didn't worry about life's quirks. Still, knowing that he was under investigation didn't exactly serve as a feather bed for his nerves. It was doubtful that Williamson could have discovered anything in so short a time. It would take a month or longer, the mail being what it was.

Nobody stopped him. He didn't see Sheriff Williamson or any other lawmen. He bought his ammunition and groceries and had loaded his saddlebags when he saw them. His heart froze. Emerging from a restaurant were the Clatchetts and Bolding. The Clatchetts were wearing long, yellow, range-style slickers for wet weather. Bolding was togged in a neat suit and he looked every bit the lawyer.

The Clatchetts saw him at the same moment, and Jeeter went for his pistol. Ivor's hand flicked out and stopped Jeeter's draw.

Keely trotted Thorny over to the gang, and Ivor greeted him with a mean smile.

"Well, well," he said.

"I want to kill all of you," Keely told him.

"You should have let me shoot him," Jeeter growled.

"And have the law on us?" Ivor shook his head.

"We don't want that," Bolding agreed.

"Why would you want to kill us?" Ivor inquired with sly innocence.

"You know why."

"For the murder of those unfortunate Mossmans?" Ivor clicked his tongue. "Why, fellow, I believe you are the one who is wanted."

Keely nodded. "I thought you'd turned

that around, but if you go to the sheriff here about it, I'll tell all I know."

"What do you know?"

"That you probably forged papers showing Cy Mossman sold the ranch to you."

For a second Ivor Clatchett lost his assurance. "How could you prove that? Nobody knows—"

Bolding interrupted: "Shut up, Ivor. You're right. Nobody knows. He's bluffing."

Keely's face was stiff with hate. "That's right, Bolding, I bluffed. But I got what I wanted—information.   Sometimes,   in poker, two pair will beat three of a kind if you catch a stupid player. You're stupid, Ivor. How many more murders did you commit, and how many forged bills of sale have you and this slime, Bolding, written out?"

"Nobody knows except you," Ivor said coolly, regaining his composure.

"Wrong."

"Wrong?"

"I've let others know what I think. If something happens to me with you in the area, people will start looking into your doings."

"You're bluffing again."

"Maybe. Maybe not."

"We'll get you," Jeeter cut in. "You're my meat, mister."

"Tell you what," Keely said. "I live up the beach about a mile. Come for me." He described the location of his cabin.

Ivor snickered. "We'll be there, fellow. Oh, yes, we'll be there. I don't believe for a minute you told anybody about us. But if you have, it's the word of a saddle bum against ours." A cynical smile passed over Ivor's lips. "We're respectable citizens."

Keely nudged his horse forward a bit. Then he shot out a pointed boot. The tip caught Ivor just under the chin, and the man sprawled backward into the grimy street.

"That's an invitation you can't refuse," Keely said bitterly.

Ivor struggled to his feet, cursing. Jeeter drew his pistol again, his eyes bright with anticipation. At that moment Sheriff Williamson appeared. He witnessed Ivor brushing himself off and cursing, and saw the red welt on his jaw.

"Arrest that man," Ivor screeched. "He assaulted me for no reason."

Williamson ignored Ivor. Instead, he said to Jeeter, "Put that gun away or I'll arrest you for threatening an unarmed man." He turned to Keely, asking in a heavily sarcastic voice, "You *are* unarmed?"

"Of course."

Jeeter slid his weapon back into its holster.

"Arrest him, I say," Ivor shouted.

"Hardly, fellow," Williamson said. "You men had a disagreement and it looks like you got the worst of it." He shrugged. "If I threw every man into jail who got into a fight, I'd have to build one bigger than the White House in Washington, D.C. This here is logger's country, friend, and they have fights just for the fun of it."

But Williamson wasn't letting Keely off. "As for you," he said, "you have twenty-four hours to get out of the country. I've had enough of you."

With that, he turned round and left.

"Come for me," Keely said to the gang. "You know where I live, but you heard the sheriff. By this time tomorrow I got to be gone. Come for me."

Then he, too, departed, leaving a yellow knot of hate glaring after him. He had no doubt that the Clatchett gang would come.

Chapter Five

I vor Clatchett had rented an office in a hotel. It was completely furnished with desk, lamps, chairs, file cabinets, spittoons—all the essentials. Ivor wanted it that way. Wherever he was in the world, he liked to have an office. It gave him a place from which to operate and a sense of belonging. An office also put him in higher standing with the town's business and professional people. An office proved he was not a fly-by-night, hip-pocket operator. He was settled, and, as the banks found out, well fixed. Ivor always deposited plenty of money in the banks, because he knew that among money men there were no secrets. The word spread and the respect he wanted soared. Respect was a good shield in his business.

Lyle Bolding had his own office in another part of town. It was best that way. Bolding was Ivor's lawyer, but as part of the shield, Bolding also represented other clients. It didn't pay for the folks to see the two of them too cozy.

It had never been Ivor's plan to keep the Mossman property. When he left Oregon, he had had several offers from the big ranchers who wanted the ground. Rangeland was disappearing and open land brought huge prices. Ivor had left the big boys dangling. The longer they had to sweat, the sweeter the pot. Ivor clapped in delight, and then he looked at his hands, and wondered about them. They, especially his right one, had the artist's touch. It could forge signatures and documents so that nobody could tell them from the real thing. He had signed the names of other men and even women to many documents, and he took pride in the writing of a phony bill of sale. He wrote in a wide, Elizabethan scroll, quite original and stylish. He signed his own name in the scroll but was quite businesslike when he forged the writing of others. Papers made up by him, under Bolding's guidance, were workmanlike, including the signature of the man he'd "bought" the property from.

Over the past few years, Ivor had been forced to kill several ranchers and their families when they proved bullheaded. First, he tried to buy them out at reduced prices. Sometimes that worked, but if not, as in the Mossman incident... well, there was no other way. Ivor Clatchett got what he wanted one way or another.

It had been a simple matter to predate the bill of sale for the Mossman property. And having that bum McGuire to blame for the murders was one of those great strokes of luck that sometimes occur. He'd told the law in Placer that he and his brothers had gone out to help the Mossmans pack their belongings—only too happy to, people helped one another in this wilderness—when he surprised the killer. It was obvious what had happened. Mossman had been murdered for the money, and the others had to be done away with as well. Leave no witnesses. He and his brothers had given chase, but the man was slippery, probably an experienced criminal, and he'd escaped. The law in Placer seemed satisfied with that account.

It had all worked out neatly. He got the property at a cost of a few bullets. Of course he'd have to split the profits with his brothers and Bolding, but his share, as leader, would be the largest. The others, including Bolding, were worker bees. They carried out his ideas. Of them all, Bolding was the most valuable, with his legal training, but his brothers had their good points too. Not many men were so eager to kill as they, even if Jeeter did hedge a little over the Mossman children. Jeeter was still miffed, but he'd come around. He always did.

There was just one kink in the rope and that was McGuire. Who would have thought that they'd meet up here in the middle of nowhere? Still, it was a happy coincidence. Now they could get him and the matter would be closed.

The door was pushed open and Bolding entered. He took a chair and came right to the point:

"What about him?"

"We'll have to kill him."

"Seems too easy. He practically handed us a gun."

"Remember, there are six of us to his one. And the sheriff didn't seem to think much of him. That's in our favor."

"Yeah." Bolding rubbed his smooth chin. "We can chance it. We have to get rid of that man. But when?"

"The sheriff gave him twenty-four hours to leave, so we'll have to get him in the morning. I want to, uh, see some timber up his way."

Bolding looked at Ivor. "We'd better slow down, speaking of that. We've already picked up quite a bit of timberland."

"We work fast."

"Too fast, Clatchett. We'd better slow down. I'm getting funny looks from the land recorder. He doesn't like it. Too many people are selling out too cheap."

Ivor's face suddenly shaped into the visage of a tiger on the hunt. "I'll say when to slow down, Bolding. We're getting ours while the getting is good. Lots of timber is for sale and I want my share. Of course" —he drummed his fingers on the desk—"if you want out...?"

Bolding   studied   his   client,   then

shrugged. "All right. We get McGuire in the morning, then?"

"Yes. He'll shoot at us for trespassing, and we'll have to fire back in self-defense."

Bolding snorted his doubt. "Six to one is self-defense?"

"What difference does that make? When he opens fire, how are we to know if there's one assailant or a dozen?"

"Yeah."

And so the script was written. The players were ready, as far as Clatchett was concerned.

At the cabin, Keely knew that he'd set the stage, and he prepared for his part. He loaded a pack with supplies and tied it on Thorny's back behind the saddle. He had no idea when the gang would arrive, and Thorny would have to be ready to spring out of there instantly.

"I'm going to leave saddle and all on you, my friend," Keely told the horse. "But that's life. We all carry extra burdens sometimes."

He checked his weapons and shells. There were two hundred rounds, enough to stand off a band of marauding Dolamish

Indians. He waited all the rest of the day, and spent an intense night deciphering creaks in the forest and scuffles along the beach. The sounds amounted to no more than wind and waves, but that didn't ease the tension.

When the sun rose the next morning, Keely cooked a large breakfast with plenty of coffee. Who knew? This could be his last meal for a while . . . or forever. He had just finished his second cup of black coffee when he heard them.

The cabin was set back several hundred feet from the beach. It was surrounded by a cape of evergreen trees and brush so closely grown that it was difficult to see for any distance. Keely was counting on that natural cover.

By the sound of them the Clatchetts had found the path leading to the cabin without trouble. They made no attempt at being quiet, arrogantly confident of their superior numbers. Besides, Keely guessed, they had committed so many killings without getting hurt that the gang felt invincible by now. *Bloody bunch,* Keely thought grimly. It didn't take much to murder a child.

He picked a place behind a large tree and lay flat. He was completely hidden from the trail. He checked his weapons, then waited. His heart was beating hard. This was the moment he had dreamed about for all too long.

The gang was now so close that Keely could hear their conversation.

"You should've got that bum, Jeeter," Ivor complained. "We wouldn't be wasting time here now."

"He was as slippery as one of these here slugs," Jeeter whined.

Ivor growled something, but the matter was dropped.

There was a sudden, coarse giggle followed by Jeeter's scratchy voice: "I say we ought to take 'im and just hang 'im from one of these here trees, eh? Be fun to watch his eyes bug out."

You slimy snake, Keely thought viciously. Moments later he saw them single-filing up the trail. Ivor was first, followed by Bolding. Then, in order, came Morey, Sag, Jeeter, and Turk. Keely aimed his rifle at Jeeter. He wanted Jeeter and Turk, the child killers, first. The brass bead of the .44's front sight nested squarely in the center of the V of the back sight, and both were lined up perfectly with Jeeter's bobbing chest.

But just as Keely squeezed the trigger, Jeeter stumbled. The .44 blasted but the lead missed. Cursing, Keely levered another shell into the barrel and fired at Turk. Turk howled and jumped a foot off the ground. He came down on his back, arms and legs flailing. "That dirty dog!" he screamed. "I'm dead!"

The mortally wounded man went into a writhing death struggle. His boots rapped a diminishing rhythm on the soft ground until they were still.

In the meantime the gang had splayed out like a wave breaking on cliffs. Keely fired rapidly, taking two shots at Sag Clatchett just as he dived behind a tree. The man screeched and clawed at both his chest and groin. Like Turk before him he cried, "Ivor, he got me too! Blast! Blast it all."

Once again there were sounds of the death struggle, rustling like moth wings in the forest, and then it was quiet. Keely changed positions and found shelter behind another large tree and waited. He was, for the moment, in command of the situation. The gang had no idea of his exact position. Nor did they know if he was alone or had allies.

The Clatchetts did know about the waiting game, however, and the silence deepened. Keely could almost hear the forest breathe, it was so quiet. A black and white magpie fluttered overhead, examining Turk's still form with a shiny eye. A crow squawked from the top of a cedar, and other birds flew to see what the excitement was about. They set up a lively racket over the deathly stillness below.

The element of surprise was gone, though. Keely had hoped to take out at least three, but only two fell. Still, they had fallen permanently, and that wasn't bad. It had been six to one, now it was four. He saw the tip of Turk's scuffed boot rising over the sunken edge of the trail, and he thought of the Mossman children. *Wish I could have gotten you a piece at a time!* he raged to himself. *You should have suffered much more, child killer!*

If the gang could wait, Keely would not. Waiting was a dangerous game. It gave the enemy time to slip around him, to plan.

Time sent reports of the shots to Angeles law, telling that something was happening. It was time to get things going. Without rising he tossed a stick downtrail toward the beach. It whistled through the air and dropped into the brush with a raspy clatter.

Instantly four guns boomed, giving away the location of their owners. Keely leaped to his feet and fired at a thin face. It belonged to Morey Clatchett. The man yelped and crashed back, his cheeks pierced and bleeding.

From the corner of his eye Keely caught another movement. He fired just as Ivor pulled his own trigger. Keely heard Clatchett's lead whisper an ominous tune so close to his ear that he ducked, but he saw Ivor jerk away. Jeeter blasted several shots from behind his tree.

Keely ducked low and readied his .44. He expected to see all four come charging at once, and he prepared to make a last stand, but the forest subsided once more into a ghostly silence—the eerie calm of battle after the fight. The crows and magpie had departed, but into the silence came a sound that brought a thin-lipped grin to Keely. Ivor moaned in pain.

"Did I get you?" Keely called, feeling safe behind a giant fir. "I hope it hurts a lot, you pig. I hope you bleed a lot, like the Mossmans. Remember Marcy?"

As Keely also remembered, grief and rage took over his well-balanced fighting spirit. He jumped up and fired again and again, firing wildly, firing at anything that moved and didn't move, until the woods roared for him to stop. But he did not stop until the hammer of his rifle clicked on an empty chamber. And then he stopped, but he drew his pistol, and stood in plain sight, daring his foes to make themselves visible. Keely, at that point, did not care if he lived or died. He had only one purpose—to kill the Clatchetts and Bolding.

Shots were returned, and Keely felt a sting in his left shoulder. He dived for cover and the shots stopped. His wound was slight, and he felt better for his outburst.

"Surprised you, didn't I?" he shouted. "You didn't expect this. No women here, Ivor. No children, Jeeter. You people and your pet dog, Bolding, are up against a man now."

The groans of Ivor indicated that the man was paying little attention. Keely heard him gasp and mutter, "I got to get a doctor or I'll bleed to death."

Keely resisted an impulse to race at the voice and kill its owner. If he did, he would surely be downed by the others, and his job would be only half finished. He resisted and listened.

"Tie this around that leg," Bolding said. "Above the hole to stop the bleeding." Then he added bitterly, "You mean we're going to leave that man alive, that *witness?*"

"Listen." Ivor's reedy voice was faint. "If we don't leave, I won't have to worry about him, not ever again."

"We can't just let him kill two of us and then get away."

"Then *you* go after him, fella. I'm getting to a doctor while I still got life."

Bolding muttered something that Keely couldn't hear, and so he called out, "Are you yellow, Bolding? How about you, child-killer Jeeter? Step out. You and I, a fair duel, eh?"

The gang ignored the invitation. Keely heard Ivor mutter, "He can't get away. These mountains are a trap. We can get men to watch for him to come out, and he's done for." Ivor groaned. "I think an artery or something has been cut. That there hole is pumping blood to beat the devil."

Keely listened to some thrashing around. It grew fainter, and he knew that the four were retreating to the beach. It was not Keely's intention to let them go, but first he had two things to do.

He dodged through the trees and found Turk's body. The man's open eyes were glazed in death. "I wish you'd been Jeeter," he said through clenched teeth, "but I'll get him, brother."

He then searched out the body of Sag, making certain that he, too, was dead. Sag lay lifeless, his death face a mask of pain.

"Not until all of you terrible people are dead will I rest," Keely whispered. "I swear that."

Grasping his reloaded rifle, he slipped through the forest, running for the beach. By now, he hoped, the four would be on shore. They would make good targets in the open. His hopes were suddenly interrupted when Morey plunged upright in front of him, his face bloody from Keely's lead.

He lifted his rifle. "Got you. Ivor said you'd maybe be along."

Keely plunged into Morey like a rampaging grizzly bear. Morey's rifle went off harmlessly, and he crumpled beneath Keely's weight. Keely struck with his own rifle, a swift uppercut catching the man on the jaw. Morey's face, already a broken mess, buckled, and he screamed as Keely brought the rifle butt down on his head. Morey fell straight down like a rock from a mountaintop and he never moved.

Keely didn't know whether Morey was dead. He didn't pause to see. He wanted the others most of all and he rushed on. As he neared salt water, a wave of excited voices reached him. He recognized one as belonging to Sheriff Williamson. Angeles law was present.

Keely stopped, well hidden from view, but he saw the beach clearly. Bolding and Jeeter were staggering under Ivor's weight. Bolding was yelling at the lawmen, of whom there were four: "That fellow's a madman! He opened up on us for no reason at all. He's killed two of us." Bolding glanced at the woods, right at Keely without seeing him in the trees. "Maybe three. I just heard another shot."

Keely drew a bead on Ivor Clatchett's back and held the bead for a count of three breaths. If he shot now, the law would know where he was. That would be bad, because chances were that they knew the woods better than he. If he wanted to do a complete job, if he wanted to get all the gang, he couldn't chance shooting Ivor, and if he wanted to escape, he was going to need all the head start possible.

It was difficult to let the .44 down, but Keely did so slowly. There was too much to lose. Besides, he had no quarrel with the law. With the lawless, yes, but not with these officers. It was time to make a run for it. Maybe a Wyatt Earp or a Doc Holliday would have fought it out, taking the chance that they'd get all their targets, but they were professional gunmen. Keely McGuire was an amateur in the business. An ordinary man. He had no desire to hang for killing scum, either, and if he were taken alive, he would surely hang, as Jeeter so joyfully wished.

Run away to fight another day. Good advice.

He raced back to the cabin and leaped on the back of Thorny. Dodging branches, he guided the horse through dense brush and devil's club, and he allowed himself a terrible smile. His shoulder stung, but he had not done so badly. He would do even better in times to come. He closed his eyes and saw the pale face and bloody hair of Marcy.

"I'll get them," he whispered. "I'll get them all, my love."

Chapter Six

Keely had scouted the land as a defense maneuver when he went up-coast for target practice. His effort didn't amount to much. The reason was the country itself. The thick forest, an entanglement of fallen trees and brush, made a difficult passage for Thorny. Nature had created a jungle to halt both the inquisitive and acquisitive.

That much Keely had learned. So, instead of heading straight back into the hills, he urged Thorny to a river that he'd discovered. The water was clear and not deep for the most part, and Keely put his horse into it.

"Just take it easy, boy," he whispered, "and we won't slip on the rocks."

He didn't listen for pursuit. It was impossible to hear anything above the rush of the river, anyway. As far as he was concerned, it was distance that counted, and he stretched it out as quickly as possible. The river proved treacherous. At times Thorny plunged chest deep into a pool of scattering trout. At times it was so shallow that water barely covered his hooves.

After fighting the cold current for hours, both Keely and his faithful Thorny were soaked, but they were in higher country. The forest, still enriched by trees that would make a logger's heart pound, was losing some of the evil underbrush. Keely left the river and dismounted. Thorny was weary, his hooves sore from the balancing he'd had to perform between river boulders. Keely led the horse and continued on foot.

Though the going was better, it was always uphill. There were no fields or flats but uphill only, and Keely was tempted to rest a dozen times. His legs ached and his lungs were raw, but he didn't rest. His plan was to get far into the mountains, into the heartland of the spires that didn't merely touch the sky but looked down on it.

Darkness came so suddenly that Keely was caught off guard. He cursed. He should have been ready. It was mid-August and darkness closed in earlier every day. It dropped over them like a trapper's net, and the two were stopped in their tracks.

A fire was too dangerous, so while Thorny munched on what grasses he could sniff out, Keely ate hardtack and cold jerky. Then he wrapped himself in a blanket and spent a sleepless night listening. His ears would tell him what his eyes couldn't. There were men after him who would not let the darkness stop them. They could find their way in the mountains and would navigate through the perils of night. They might even anticipate him and wait at some high pass ahead. If they sighted him, a man now wanted in both Oregon and Washington, a man of murderous intent, it was possible that the law would shoot first and ask questions afterward.

The next morning a thick fog had settled over the land. Keely blessed it. He traveled on Thorny's capable back as swiftly as possible, and the going was always up.

He reached timberline and still kept spiraling upward, aiming always at the deep backcountry. He would not be satisfied until he was so far back into the mountains that the sky would kiss the horizon.

The fog lingered and Keely could have hugged it, because visibility was a hundred yards at best. If the posse was around, the riders would have to be very close to see him. He was a mere rock in the quarry, and invisible nearly. But he kept his rifle ready. Though the fog choked off sound, like fingers on a throat, Thorny's hooves and saddle leather creaking did make a commotion. Keely couldn't be sure how far the muffled noises could be heard, but he was ready. All he had to do was cock the hammer and pull the trigger.

If the law was present, it missed him. He coiled through rugged crags for two days and was never challenged. He saw only a black bear, a cougar, and several elk. But their challenges were in passing only. A snarl from the cougar, a sniff from the nearsighted bear, a stiffening among the elk.

On the third day, toward evening, he pitched his tent for the first time. It was a wall tent, one he could move around in, and he set up a sort of permanent camp—"sort of," he told himself, because nothing was permanent for him now.

The camp was high but just at timberline, because he needed firewood. He seemed to be in some kind of pass, because the ground stretched out in either direction to disappear like waterfalls dropping off. Later he would choose a higher post, but he wanted a fire and he dared build a small one here. He brewed coffee and luxuriated in the warmth of the crackling flames. He allowed himself to relax, but always with his rifle at hand. Thorny had plenty of food, for the grass was still green. The horse seemed to sense that this was close to the end of the trail, and he munched slowly, juicing his molars at a leisurely pace.

Keely laid low for two days. He didn't have any plan beyond what circumstances had prepared for him. He let the hours unfold, bringing what they would, but never once letting his guard down. He scouted the region, seeking escape routes should they be necessary. At the end of his seeking, he felt that if he were found here, no other place in the mountains would be safe. This was as deep and as far as he could go. Any direction from this was out again. He was at the center of his region, the heartland.

On the sixth day, with grub running low, Keely decided to chance a shot. Elk were grazing in a short valley a thousand feet below camp. One would be his. He rode Thorny to within stalking distance, crept closer on foot, and downed an animal with a single shot.

After butchering his kill he loaded most of it on Thorny and climbed back to camp. As he approached, something didn't seem right. He had lived so much at nerve's edge the past few weeks that his perceptions were extra keen. Something was wrong in camp.

Keely dropped Thorny's reins, and while the horse stayed put he crept up on the tent. He flung the flap open to behold a thin Indian with a spoon in his hand. He had been helping himself to cold beans.

"Who are you?" Keely demanded, rifle ready.

For an answer the Indian flung himself at Keely. Taken by surprise, Keely tumbled back, the Indian on top and swinging with hard fists. Keely rolled from under his adversary easily, and with a few blows subdued him. At first Keely thought that it was some kind of ruse. His opponent was pretending defeat and would strike again without warning.

He was correct. The Indian did attack again, but once more was quickly subdued. Then Keely realized that the man was really stealing food and not pretending. He was weak, possibly starving. He was so thin that his bones stuck out through his taut, dark skin.

Suddenly the Indian stood erect, stepped back, and bared his chest.

"You do it now," he said.

"Do what?"

"You kill me."

"Kill you?" Keely was astonished. "For taking a few beans? Why?"

"The Dolamish kill slaves for stealing."

"But," Keely said, his voice gentle, "you are not a slave here. You are a free man. Besides," he added, "there are no slaves anymore. We fought a war to get rid of slavery. My father died in that war."

The Indian's eyes were dark, made

darker by hunger. "I know of no war like that. The Dolamish still have slaves." And the emaciated figure, scarcely thicker through the middle than a small birch tree, threw some proud words: "We Tlingits, we have slaves too." He spat. "More than the Dolamish! The Tlingits are rich." He pointed to his bared chest. "I am ready."

"Well, I'm not." Keely lifted the pot of beans that had been cooked nearly a week before. "You eat," he said.

The Indian was doubtful. Obviously he was wondering whether Keely's offer was a trick.

"You kill me," he insisted. "Don't do Josh Deerface a foolish thing."

"Eat," Keely ordered, handing the spoon to the Indian.

A speck of hope flashed through the night shadowing the Indian's eyes.

"I eat, then maybe you kill me later?"

"I am not going to kill you."

"If the Dolamish catch me, they will kill us both. I'm their property. You steal me, they think."

"They can think what they want. Eat."

Hesitantly, Josh Deerface took the spoon. He dipped into the pot and lifted a spoonful of beans to his mouth. He snatched at them as a hungry dog would snatch at a bone. His dark eyes were slitted, wary, but he ate. As he ate he lost his apprehension, and after a few mouthfuls was gobbling the beans frantically.

"Take it easy," Keely advised. "They aren't going away."

A faint grin appeared on the Indian's face. "Oh, yes, they sure are." And he snatched another mouthful. "Kaupy?"

Keely had learned enough Chinook jargon, a language common to both whites and Indians in the Northwest, to know "kaupy" meant coffee.

"I'll get my horse first," he said. "Then we'll have kaupy."

After Thorny was unloaded, Keely made a small fire and put the coffee on. Josh Deerface watched while he warmed himself before the fire. Keely opened a can of tomatoes and gave them to the Indian. Josh ate silently, and when the can was empty it served as a cup for the coffee.

Josh took a sip and set the hot can down. He blew on his fingers and grinned again. "Kaupy bites."

Keely found himself admiring this strange person who was willing to give up his life one minute and could joke about hot fingers the next.

"You say you're an escaped slave?"

"Yes. I get away from the Dolamish. They are good warriors, but don't beat Josh Deerface up here." He tapped his head. "I'm pretty smart."

"How come you were a slave if you're so smart?"

"Two summers ago I killed a man in my tribe. He came at me with knife. I don't know why. Crazy, I think. But I took the knife from him and killed him instead." Josh frowned at the unpleasant memory. "Anyway, that is not good in my tribe. The chiefs think I kill this man because I am jealous." Josh's voice, which was soft and smooth by nature, took on shy overtones. "Woman I like likes him better, you know?" Josh sipped his coffee. "But that wasn't it. He came at me and I get him. The chiefs sent for me. They wanted to kill me maybe, an eye for an eye. I don't know. I didn't want to know, either. So I left in a hurry. I take canoe and go far. Too far. I got caught by Dolamish while sleeping. They make me a slave. They don't like the Tlingits. We beat them in war long, long ago, but they don't forget."

Keely listened with interest. Here was a man like himself. Josh was wanted by Indian laws and he was wanted by the white man's laws. Neither of them was guilty of a crime, but circumstances made it seem that they were. They were one of a kind—fugitives.

"Where are you going now?" he asked.

Josh shrugged. "I'll be your slave."

"No."

"Then I go outside." He pointed to the valleys below. "I'll see if white men come for you. Josh pay for his food."

Keely was surprised. "You know about them?"

"Sure. All the Indians here, even the stupid Dolamish, know about your fight with those men. I have seen it."

"You saw it?"

"I was near your cabin." Josh offered no explanation as to why he was near the cabin. "I saw you fight." His face glowed with admiration. "You're a good warrior. Many against one. I saw that. You kill two. Very brave. Good fighting."

Keely was touched by the man's direct talk. His people lived under the rule of an eye for an eye, a law as old as mankind. Here was Josh about to do him a favor and risk his life doing it in order to pay for his food. If the Dolamish were lurking about, they would kill him, and Josh knew it. But he would pay for his food. Josh Deerface was Keely's kind of man.

"No," Keely said, "you stay here with me. I have an extra blanket. You watch when I sleep, and I'll watch when you sleep."

A smile of pure joy stole over Josh's face. Keely was reminded of a child receiving a present, one he had always wanted. But the joy changed to a frown.

"The Dolamish will come for me," he said. "You will have to give me back to them."

"No," Keely said. "I won't."

"They will kill you, then."

"No," Keely repeated. "They won't. You stay and that's final."

"Final? What do you mean? I don't know all your white words."

"I mean—you stay, that is all."

Josh Deerface understood that. He nodded.

It was growing dark. Keely gave Josh a blanket. "You rest," he said, "while I get the meat covered with a tarp."

Josh didn't answer. Wrapped in his blanket, he had fallen asleep while sitting up. The firelight flickered on his gaunt face. There was a mixture of manly strength and childlike innocence in the face, but Keely knew that he'd gained an ally. Heaven knew he needed one.

And what about the Dolamish? How could they ever find him up here? It was impossible.

Chapter Seven

Keely sensed they were there. Gripping his Colt .44, he stepped out of the tent. A dozen Dolamish formed a semicircle in front of him. They were dressed in both white and Indian clothing—derby hats, cotton shirts and vest, deerskin trousers and moccasins.

"What do you want?" he asked as if he didn't know.

One of them pointed to Josh as he emerged from the tent. "Our property," he said.

The man was squat and bullnecked. He had a broad, blunt face and unfriendly, bleak eyes.

"And who are you?"

"I am Chief Blackax." The chief gestured impatiently. "Give him to us."

"I'll go," Josh said.

"No," Keely said. "You belong to me now."

Josh gave him a glance, then stepped back.

"We take him," Chief Blackax said. He advanced, his men following.

Keely didn't want trouble with them. He had enough trouble. "Tell you what," he said. "I'll give you a pound of tobacco and two pounds of kaupy for him."

Blackax shook his heavy head. "Not enough. Tlingit good slave. Worth much."

"I'll throw in two boxes of hardtack, a pound of sugar, and"—he reached into his pocket and pulled out a jackknife—"this."

The Dolamish chief hesitated. It was his decision to make, because Josh had been his slave. He nodded a few times, but as he did so, Keely noted the man's eyes slyly roving around the campsite.

Keely raised his .44 and shot the chief's derby off. It went sailing downhill. The chief, shaken and wide-eyed, clutched his own rifle. But Keely had the drop on him.

"If you hope to come back tonight to get it all, plus Josh Deerface too, you are mistaken. Go."

"I want my slave."

"Go at once, or I'll break your arms and legs." Keely nodded at the warriors, most of whom were armed with bows and arrows though a few carried rifles. "Maybe you can kill us, but I will get you first."

Chief Blackax's face flushed full red. He was being faced down by a white man. No humiliation could be greater.

"I want what you pay—kaupy and knife and all that."

"You don't get it now. Go." Keely aimed at a rock and shot. The rock exploded. "Or I do that to you too."

Scowling, his face a road map to vengeance, Blackax said something to his men, and then they all retreated. They were not on horseback. Keely had noted that these Indians, being seafaring men, owned few horses.

"They will come back," Josh warned.

"Let them. Let's have breakfast."

What worried Keely were the shots that had been fired. Had anyone else heard them? The mountains tossed echoes back and forth like a storm tosses waves of the ocean.

After they'd eaten he said, "Let's have a

look to see if anybody is coming." He pointed northwest. "I'll go that way, you go south. If you see anybody at all, come back here, but don't let them see you."

"See me?" Josh was indignant. "Nobody sees Josh, not even mountain goats, who see over the end of the earth."

Keely nodded. He had offended a man who was probably more skilled at traveling stealthily than any white. Josh's pained expression amused him but he was careful not to show it.

Keely waved a hand and departed. He was gone most of the morning, saw nothing to cause alarm, and returned. Josh was waiting by the tent.

"Did you see anything?" Keely asked.

"No, but Dolamish are near."

"How do you know?"

"I smell them."

"Smell them?"

"Yes." Josh looked puzzled. "Don't you?"

Keely shook his head, and his face showed doubt.

"You will see," Josh insisted. "They will come back. They want me. They want you. You have disgraced their big chief."

"Too bad," Keely said with a grin. "He's a liar."

The rest of the day was spent in talking and keeping watch. Keely learned from Josh that the Tlingits were the most feared of warriors and they had the most beautiful women. The Tlingits were also among the few Indians not enslaved by the Russians.

"When Russians owned the North," Josh said, "we were too strong for them. We fought them. The Russians didn't make Tlingits work. We traded instead."

Whether Josh was simply bragging or telling the truth, Keely didn't know, but he saw no reason to doubt the man. In his turn, when Josh questioned Keely about the fight with the Clatchetts, Keely found that he couldn't explain it. He was still too angry and emotional to express his thoughts clearly, and so he changed the subject to his ranch in Wyoming.

"Bad, huh?" Josh asked, not referring to Wyoming.

"Yes," Keely said, "very bad," knowing what Josh meant.

They discussed moving camp for

safety's sake. In the end they discarded the idea.

"The Dolamish will always know where we are," Josh said. "Why work at all that moving when it will do no good?"

So they stayed. Night fell, and with it their caution rose. Something was going to happen.

Josh heard them first.

"They slip around like weasels," he whispered. "We'd better not stay in the tent."

Keely agreed, and they took up positions behind some nearby rocks. A few minutes later Keely made out a shadow darker than the night. The shadow was joined by others, and a few seconds later orange flashes bloomed from the shadows like flowers, and rifles boomed. The Dolamish were firing into the tent. Keely fired from his rock, as did Josh, who had the pistol. The shadows disappeared. Keely didn't want to kill any of the Indians. That would be bad, resulting in a blood feud. All he wanted was to chase them off.

"Don't hit them!" Keely cried.

Josh was blazing away in the night, and

the pistol flared like a Fourth of July Roman candle.

"I must kill them," Josh said. "They are sons of dogs."

The Dolamish yelled and screamed fiercely, and discharged their rusty rifles and bows and arrows. Bedlam shook the mountains like crazy thunder.

It was over in minutes. Keely heard Chief Blackax yell something, and there was silence. The night turned treacherously quiet, like a prowling snake.

Josh crouched next to Keely. "I think," he whispered, "that they are out of shells."

"But they didn't fire that much."

"Dolamish don't have many shells. They are not rich in white man's things."

Keely reloaded the six-gun and rifle, and settled down to wait. The two remained hidden until dawn, but the Indians did not return.

"The chief is ashamed," Josh said. "He will think of some way to get back at you."

"I can't worry about that." Keely shivered, for the morning was cold. "Let's make a fire and eat."

Keely cooked breakfast and then made some decisions. They would move their tent but keep it near the forest because they needed firewood. It looked as if he and Josh were going to be in the hills for a long time.

They moved camp ten miles away and settled just below the timberline. Every day they expected trouble, but none came. The snow arrived one night, and it was deep. The wind came too, like a ferocious playmate, and tossed the snow around, piling up drifts. Keely and Josh hunkered in the tent and built a fire inside on the ground. Then the wind died and the snow stopped, and the sun came out and melted the snow, but Keely knew that this was a warning. If he and Josh were to remain in the hills, they would need a lot of supplies.

"Otherwise," Keely said, "we'll be eating snowballs and pepper."

"Snow bad, pepper good," Josh, who liked spices, observed.

"I'll go to Dungeness, " Keely said. "I'll get a packhorse and load him with what we need."

"I go too."

"No. I'll leave the rifle. If anybody comes, run for it. Don't fight them—run away. We will meet somewhere." Keely pointed due east. "Over there. The rifle will get you food."

"I go too."

"You are stubborn."

"Yes."

"I am more stubborn than you, and I am stronger and you are my slave. You will do as I say."

Josh grinned. "You've told me two times I am your slave. Am I that?"

Keely was embarrassed. "Well, no, but I go alone. It will be easier. They will recognize you, maybe."

Josh's grin widened until he looked like a happy cat. "What about you, redbeard?"

Josh was right, so Keely shaved his beard off.

"Are you the same man?" Josh exclaimed.

"I look different, right?"

"There is no face like yours."

Keely wasn't sure if that was a compliment, but he ended up going alone. It wasn't difficult to find Dungeness, because he could see the town after traveling north several miles. The little port seemed like a handful of scattered rice in the distance.

As he neared town he was unaware of the girl who watched him. Tanada knew that the tall man on the horse was Keely even though he had no beard. She could tell by his eyes and nose and the way he carried himself. She could also tell by his horse. She knew about the fight on the beach and the two dead men, but she hadn't known if Keely was still alive. She was glad he was.

There was in Dungeness a character known as Shanghai Masterson. He was pure thug, the offspring of criminal parents. He had grown up outside the law and remained outside the law, though his activities were smoothly covered. His main business seemed to be timber, but his most lucrative one was the procurement of sailors for needy skippers. Sailors often jumped ship for one reason or another, leaving them short of enough men to run them. It was Masterson who filled that need. He controlled a gang who roamed the streets, looking for unwilling prospects to spend two years before the mast. Masterson's profits were one hundred percent since he never paid for his merchandise. Strangers in town were preferred.

Masterson's men were doing their job when Keely arrived in town. They had cornered a gent in a back alley and were methodically beating him into an unconscious state. This was the preferred method of procurement, since a conscious man would yell bloody murder as he was being carted aboard an eager skipper's ship. It took a lot of men to hoist sails and unload cargo.

Masterson himself was taking part in this operation. He was a brutal man who enjoyed using his fists and sometimes picked fights just for the fun of it. He was a red-faced, rawboned fellow, strong as a grizzly bear. When Keely saw him and his associates pounding on their prospective goods, he didn't like it. He believed in fair play. He didn't know if the victim was a good or bad man. He didn't know who Masterson was, or any of the others. He simply didn't like seeing one man try to hold off six, as in his battle with the Clatchetts.

"Hey!" he called out. "Even it up a little."

Nobody answered. After all, this was a money-making venture, and interference was not wanted.

"Put a cork in it," Keely shouted, "or I'll call the law."

Masterson turned at that. The gang stopped thrashing their quarry, who reeled against a wall, bloody and about done in.

"You say that about the law again," Masterson threatened, "and we'll beat *your* brains in."

"I doubt it."

"You do?"

"Yes. You and your boys are cowards. You gang up like coyotes and chew your game to bits."

With a great light of joy in his eyes, Masterson leaped at Keely. His fists, the size of coconuts, landed on Keely, punching hard. His men joined him, and their previous victim took advantage of this in-attention and fled.

The gang was expert in beating people to pulp, and before long Keely knew he'd put his foot into a trap. He was not a small man and his biceps needn't take a back-seat to anyone, but he felt his legs weaken-ing.

"Let's give him to a ship," somebody muttered.

"Good idea," Masterson howled. "We lost one, we got another."

The blows, expertly placed, increased in vigor, and Keely experienced moments of darkness. He felt no pain but was growing numb. He realized he was badly hurt and bleeding, but he fought on. He was aware that he could even die, but still he fought on. He didn't know when the blows stopped, but he did hear words vaguely: "We got to git. The law's coming and this feller's still too alive to cart along. He'll yell."

Acting from instinct, Keely managed to crawl upon Thorny and walk him from town. He didn't want to tangle with the law, either. The law in Dungeness probably knew all about him and the Clatchetts. He felt himself swaying in the saddle, and at that point he heard a woman's voice— or he thought he did, and then he lost contact with the world.

When he came to, he opened his eyes and groaned, "Where am I?"

"You are in my place." The woman's voice had returned.

Lying flat on his back, Keely tried to sit up. Hot fire and burning needles punched him back down quickly, and he lay very still. A young woman leaned over him. She had long black hair and kind brown eyes.

"Who are you?" he muttered. "One of the gang out there?"

"No," was the scornful reply. "I am Tanada."

Her face receded. It wavered and washed away. When Keely saw light again, the world was a bit more clear. Yet, when he started to sit up, the same hot fire and needles played a winning game, and he collapsed.

"What did I get into?" he mumbled through swollen lips.

"You got beat up by that skunk Masterson and his men."

Tanada leaned over him once more. This time she had a cup of hot liquid. She held his head up and put the cup to his lips. "Drink," she said. "You have not eaten in two days."

Keely swallowed. It was the worst brew

he had ever tasted and he spit it out indelicately.

"For pity's sake, what is it?"

"Juice of clams and oysters and fish heads."

"Fish heads?"

"Yes. It's good for you." A smile played on her full lips. "Give you brains, maybe."

She held the liquid to his lips once more, and there was no avoiding it. Keely was too weak to resist. It was drink or choke, and so he drank. Tanada kept the cup to his lips until all the broth was gone.

"Good," she said. "Now maybe you start to get better."

Suddenly the meaning of her words dawned on Keely. He struggled to sit up, and with her help made it. "You say I've been here two days?"

"And two nights."

"Good grief."

Keely thought a minute. The broth might not have been to his taste, but there was no doubt about its medicinal qualities. His mind was sharper, and even the fire and needles had cooled down.

"How did I get here?"

"I brought you."

"Oh?"

"I saw the fight. You should have run. I know you fought those other men at your cabin—everybody knows about that. But you should have run from Masterson."

Keely touched the sore bruises on his face. "You're right."

Tanada smiled. She was pretty, with her fine mouth and brown eyes. Her face was lighter than the Indian dark, but more tan than white. She was tall and supple, and she carried herself with a proud, straight back.

"Why did you bring me here?" Keely asked. "Aren't you afraid Masterson or the law will come looking?"

"No. They didn't see you fall from your horse. They didn't see me take you." Her eyes flashed. "Masterson would have put you on a ship."

"Oh?"

Tanada told him about the shanghaier's main occupation.

Keely whistled. Right now, he could be bouncing around far out at sea. He owed the girl much. He said to her:

"But if the law does come, the sheriff

can get you for obstructing justice—or whatever it's called here."

"I don't like the white man's law," she said. "The sheriff and others always tell me to move on, move on, but Tanada stays." She tossed her head like a free creature of the wild. "Nobody, not even the law, can tell me what to do."

Keely was able to move around after two more days. The fires and needles had diminished, but when he tried to do some real work, such as chopping wood for Tanada's rickety stove, pain sent him back to a chair. Masterson and his men had done a thorough job.

"I ought to go back and smash a few faces for this," he grumbled.

"Sure, and end up on a ship—or in jail."

It was the thought of jail that dissuaded Keely from any heroics. Jail and the curiosity of the law were things he did not want. So he grumbled and let himself heal.

After five days he felt well enough to travel again.

"I have to get back into the hills," he told Tanada. "There's a man waiting for me. He needs grub."

"Josh Deerface?"

Keely was surprised.

"Oh, I know him. We help each other sometimes."

Keely nodded. It made sense. Josh, the escaped slave, Tanada, a girl of the wilderness. What kind of life did she lead? How did she make a living? The questions must have showed in his face, because she answered them:

"I am half white, half Indian—whites call me a half-breed. My tribe doesn't want me, and the whites don't want me, either. So what do I do?" She drew herself up. "I make my own way. I don't need whites or Indians. I don't care about them if they don't care about me. I live without them."

"But if you don't like whites, why did you take care of me?"

"Because you are like me and Josh Deerface. You don't belong anywhere either. The law wants you. And the Clatchetts want you. You have to hide."

"I'm not afraid of any Clatchett!" Keely was offended.

"I did not say that. I know of your bravery. You killed two of them. But you have to watch out. They may get you in the back, yes?"

"Yes," he admitted.

"They have the law on their side now, yes?"

Keely nodded.

"So you have to hide."

"Yes."

"All right, so I will hide you from the law and the Clatchetts, and man with hair like black glass."

"Bolding."

The girl shrugged. "Names don't matter. People and how they act—that matters a lot."

Keely had to agree with that. You knew a man by his actions better than any other way.

"I make my living," Tanada went on, "by washing clothes for whites. I need whites for that much. One family was kind to me, and they taught me to read and write. I liked them, but they moved." She smiled wryly. "People move. It is like a door closing on you, isn't it?"

Keely remembered the Mossmans and Marcy. Yes, he knew about closing doors.

Tanada resumed, "So I make a little

money and I pick berries, catch fish, and shoot deer." She pointed to a scarred .25-20 caliber rifle hanging on a wall. "That's my deer getter. I get along with very little, but it is enough. Tanada is doing fine."

As Keely listened, he watched this girl who talked with her hands as well as words. She was expressive and graceful. In a way, she reminded him of Marcy. Marcy had been graceful, and she, too, had spoken expressively with her hands. But there the comparison ended. Marcy had been gentle, civilized, acquainted with the intellectual and artistic sides of life. Tanada was rough and tumble. She had never even seen a fine painting or played a musical instrument. Life had knocked her about, and yet she was surviving and, according to her standards and expectations, surviving quite well. She scorned both Indians and whites and threw their blows back with a proud toss of her head. Though not an expert on the different kinds of women, Keely knew that Tanada was a remarkable person.

He changed the subject back to its beginnings: "I have to get grub and go back to camp."

"Me too."

"You too, what?"

"I go with you."

"No," Keely said.

"Yes," Tanada said with a stubborn thrust of her chin, and Keely saw that he was going to have an argument.

Chapter Eight

Sheriff Williamson was a suspicious man. He had been in law enforcement all his working years, and entanglement with all kinds of crooks had left him with a sour outlook on mankind. He liked enforcing the law, though, and had worked in Tombstone, Dodge City, Abilene, and other western towns before putting space between himself and cattle country. No man was too virtuous to escape his scrutiny. The latest among these, in addition to Keely McGuire, were Ivor Clatchett, his skinny brothers, and the slick-haired lawyer, Lyle Bolding.

There was too much timberland coming into the hands of the Clatchett Syndicate, as it was called. There were too many people selling out cheap and heading south to avoid the northern winter. So it was said.

Williamson, obeying his acquired suspicions of everybody, took an interest in all kinds of local transactions. Timber sales were hot, and he knew from experience that when sales boomed in any commodity from land to turnpike to timber, there was room for cheating. He had made it a point to examine most bills of sale for timber property, and had noted that Ivor Clatchett's new holdings had gone to him at surprisingly low prices. They were signed by him as receiver in a large, rolling scroll, beautifully done. But it was also a signature that asserted, "Don't fool around with me."

The sheriff knew that the Clatchetts and Bolding came from Oregon, and that there had been some shady land dealings in that territory. He'd been apprised of this by Oregon lawmen, just the same as he passed relevant information back to them. The Clatchetts had been in on a number of the land transactions. Nothing illegal could be proved, because lawyer Bolding had all the right papers to prove that the land was legally purchased. Still, the prices paid were too low and foul play was suspected. The Mossman place was a case in point. The land had gone for a tenth of the going rate. And then there was the fate of the Mossmans.

Sheriff Williamson was leaving for a well-earned vacation to California. He planned to spend the winter enjoying the sublime climate and easing the creaks and rust in his joints. The Olympic Peninsula was a long way from Arizona's heat. He had no qualms about absenting himself for so long a period. His deputies would keep order. On the way back, in a few months, he would stop at Placer and look over some records there. He would examine them for Ivor Clatchett's signature. If the sales documents showed prices that were too low, he could be on to something. He didn't know quite what, but like many lawmen he played his hunches. One thing often led to another. . . .

Meanwhile, the object of Williamson's conjecture was done up to the nines in sartorial splendor. A custom-made suit and shirt, low-heeled boots from Abilene, and a cravat from Paris had turned him from a

gaunt, spindly clothes hanger into a gentle-
man of refined taste.

He was admiring himself in front of a
full-length mirror. Lyle Bolding was
watching, amused.

"You're going to rope them in, eh?" the
lawyer asked.

"They'll be eating out of my hand," was
the smug response. "This shindig I'm giving tonight should turn me into something
of a personage in this fair hamlet of the
North."

"You even talk differently—like an ad-
mirer of Shakespeare."

"A man of culture, that's me."

Bolding couldn't resist a smirk, but he
said, "All the town bigwigs will be present,
I suppose."

"Of course. If you want to cut a wide
swath, my dear Bolding, use a long ma-
chete."

"I want to say something." Bolding had
turned serious.

"Say it."

"I still think we ought to slow up on
these timber deals."

Ivor's narrow face seemed to shrink like
an eagle's claw grasping its prey. "Think

what you like," he replied in a thin voice, "but do as I say, Bolding. I want all the timber I can get while the getting's good."

"The getting might not be so good as you suppose. People are asking questions. I understand that Williamson has been snooping. We've been burying too many people, Ivor. The matter of cheap ground coming into our hands too often is causing uneasiness."

"Nobody can prove a thing, Bolding. We have papers to prove our transactions are legal."

"Sheriff Williamson—" Bolding began, but he was cut off with a snort from Ivor.

"That oaf," Ivor sneered. He cleared his throat and spat into a brass spittoon. "If he can tell the time of day, I'll die of surprise."

"Don't underestimate him. I've dealt with his kind. He's stubborn and might dig up something."

Ivor smiled happily. "Well," he said in a jovial mood, anticipating the evening's affair, "if he gets too nosy, we'll give Jeeter a little target practice. Jeeter makes the best back shots in the country."

"We've never dealt with the law quite so directly," a reluctant Bolding pointed out.

"Perhaps it's time," Ivor Clatchett purred.

"He's going away for the winter, I hear."

"Oh?" Clatchett smoothed a lapel. "Well, let's worry about him when he gets back." He pretended he was aiming a rifle and said softly, "Bam." He then stepped in front of the mirror. "Do I look all right?"

"A fashion plate."

"You're teasing, I know, but, yes, I do seem quite passable. Come on, let's go. And don't worry. All lawmen are oafs— you know that."

In another part of the country Chief Blackax was sitting on a large boulder overlooking the Strait of Juan de Fuca. He was smoking a small, smelly cigar, and his face was sullen. He was thinking of ways to get revenge on the white man and the Indian slave. He had been beaten twice by them, once with words, once with weapons. He did not like defeat. Nor was it good for him in his tribe to lose. Respect for him had diminished. The council had chided him on his retreat after the gunfight. One more defeat and he could be eliminated as leader of the Dolamish. Only the best survived as leaders.

A plan was forming. It meant he would have to deal with whites, and he didn't like to deal with them. They had not proved honest. They cheated his people whenever it was to their benefit. Right now, whites were taking timber that rightfully belonged to Dolamish and other coastal tribes. There was a time when Blackax had thought of going to war with the whites, but history had taught him a lesson. The great Nez Percé leader, Chief Joseph, had fought them and lost. With two hundred and fifty of the best warriors, he had fought two thousand whites and lost. It was a valiant fight but he had lost, and it had caused Joseph to say, "I will fight no more forever." And he never did. Chief Blackax knew about Joseph, and he knew of other white-Indian battles. The Indians had won some, but the whites won most, because there were more whites. It was as simple as that. So a war could not be won. But the peace could be lived with, and Blackax existed with the whites. He played the game of life by their rules when necessary. Still, there were Indian rules too, and these regulated his daily life. These rules could make or break him, and he did not intend that they should break him.

The chief sighed. It was not easy being headman. One had to do things one did not wish to do, but he must deal with the white men. There was one he knew he could trust, and that was Ivor Clatchett. Clatchett had lost two brothers to the man who was causing so much trouble. Blackax knew that Clatchett would hunt the killer of his brothers and kill him. That would be all that was necessary. Blackax would not have to take any direct action himself. He would tell Clatchett where that white man was, and then he could trust Clatchett to do the job. Blackax would tell the council of his plan and get credit for it, and he would once again be regarded as a wise chief. He would have gotten his revenge by using white against white. Very good.

At the other end of the social scale, far below Dolamish chiefs and upward-bound whites, were an outlaw and a half-Indian girl. They were having a heated argument. They were, in fact, shouting.

"We have no place for you up there!" Keely boomed.

"I'll make a place," was the infuriating response.

"It's not good for a woman to live with two men."

"I will make my own cabin. I will not be in your way."

"You have a life of your own here. Come with me, and you'll be a criminal too."

Tanada's dark eyes mocked him. "A life?" She swept her dark cabin with a contemptuous glance. "You call this a life? I live the best way I know, but if I leave this, I leave nothing."

"Well," Keely said with what he figured was good manly firmness, "you can't go and that's that."

A sly knowledge flitted across Tanada's face like a splinter about to do its work on an unsuspecting hand. "You intend to come here for food, don't you?"

"Yes."

"How will you get it?"

"Why, I'll just buy—"

Stark truth intruded on Keely's intended answer. He could not go back to Dungeness. He could not go to Port Angeles. Perhaps Townsend?

"No," Tanada said, sensing the direction of his thoughts. "Townsend people will look for you too. They will look for you everywhere, I think, except maybe Blyn. I can get things for you there."

Blyn was bustling, as were most coastal towns, but it was tucked off by itself. Maybe the mainstream of events had bypassed it.

"Maybe not," Tanada said, reading Keely's mind again. "But I can buy for you there. You will give me money."

Keely knew that Tanada had him. He didn't dare show his face in any community, not even Blyn.

"What do you want in return if you buy for me?"

"I want to go to the mountains."

"Blast."

The girl smiled. "Yes."

Keely gave in. Something could be worked out in the mountains, but right now he had to get going. Josh was out of food by now.

They did not waste any more time. There was permanent snow on the peaks now, and it would soon drop to Josh's level and it would get deep. Shelter must be built before that time. A tent would not be enough.

Tanada was successful. While Keely remained in the woods, she purchased a packhorse and loaded him with supplies that would be necessary for survival. These included an iron stove and an extra .44 rifle for Josh. The finished load of provisions was too much for one horse, and so Thorny, too, had to pack a load.

Keely led the way back. He wasn't sullen but he was quiet. He was puzzled by his feelings, because he was really glad that Tanada had won the argument. True, there was no place for a woman with two men, and yet he realized that these were not ordinary circumstances. Adjustments would have to be made.

Every now and then he glanced at Tanada, and what he saw brought admiration. He saw a determined spirit, a woman alone, one who didn't accept that she was supposed to roll over and play dead. She didn't know that she was supposed to be humiliated because she was half Indian. She met scoffers with scorn of her own. Keely saw beauty too. Tanada's beauty was not like the delicate features of Marcy —it was more subtle, like the evening loveliness when mountain valleys were deep and mysterious and quiet. Tanada's beauty suited her perfectly. She was a product of wilderness and reflected the spirit of wilderness.

The trip back to camp took two long days. On the way Tanada pointed out the landmarks.

"That is Spirit Gate," she said, pointing to a deep gorge. "You look at cliffs and see spirits."

Keely squinted, but all he saw were cliffs. Tanada was amused.

"White people are not good at seeing things like that," she said.

Toward evening on the second day they arrived at a high plateau above camp.

"This is Lost Pass," Keely was told. "I don't know why. It isn't lost." She laughed softly at her joke.

Keely squinted again. To the west was clear sky, to the east was the same. He supposed that a person could travel through the mountains by this pass, and he took note of the fact. But it didn't look like much to him, either.

"You know a lot about these mountains," he remarked.

"I go up here much," Tanada said. "Here I am myself. Not half white and half Indian, just me. I like that."

They dropped down into camp, where Josh greeted them with both joy and alarm.

"Why," he asked bluntly, "did you bring her?"

"She saved my life."

Josh grunted. "Pretty good reason, I guess. She will go back now?"

"No, Josh. She stays with us."

"Where will she live?"

"Shall I tell you how Tanada saved my life?"

"It doesn't matter. You are here."

Josh's lack of curiosity was typical of him, Keely had learned. Josh took things as they came. One day, perhaps, he would want to know how his life had been saved. Not now. He had more important things—

at least, more immediate things—on his mind.

"Snow come low." He pointed to the white cloth spread across the mountain-tops. "We build cabin?"

"Yes."

They started to build the next day. While one of them stood watch—they could never be sure that Blackax or the Clatchetts would not return—the other two cut logs and built the cabin. Tanada worked as hard as the men. And she knew what to do, how to handle an ax and how to place logs properly. She knew more about building a log house than Keely did, and he did not mind. He let Tanada and Josh do most of the planning while he supplied muscle. There were two rooms—a small one for Tanada and the main room.

"Waste of time," Josh grumbled. "All sleeping in the same room will save heat."

It was the way Josh had lived, Keely learned. In Josh's home village, three or four families spent their lives in one big-roomed house. Each family had a section to itself. There were no rooms or even partitions.

"Save wood that way," Josh pointed

out. "And we share what we have with each other."

"Well, Tanada will have her own room," Keely said firmly, taking that much of a part in the planning. "That's the way it will be."

Josh didn't argue. He might object to something occasionally, but he never argued. He would tease, though.

"Afraid of the girl, eh?"

"No, I'm not afraid."

"I think you are. She will take over and be the leader."

"Josh, you coyote, shut up and cut logs."

Josh grinned, but he didn't warm up to Tanada until some time had passed. He resented her, and Keely wondered about it. Three could be worse than a crowd if hostilities broke out.

Tanada worked hard, never complained, and there seemed to be a joy in her as the cabin went up. Josh must have seen the joy too, but Keely noted that it made no impression. Instead, the Tlingit was insulting.

"You cook like my father," he grumbled over Tanada's stew.

"Don't eat it, then," was the tart response.

"You snore when you sleep."

Tanada blushed. "Then don't listen."

"You are an ignorant woman."

"Are you so bright?"

Keely drew Josh aside. "What's going on here? Get nice, or—"

"Or what will you do?"

"I'll think of something."

Josh did not take Keely's warning. One evening while Keely dozed by the fire after a particularly strenuous day, Josh, who was sharpening axes, suddenly blurted out, "You, girl!"

Tanada was washing what dishes they had. She whirled swiftly, sensing trouble.

"You, girl," Josh repeated, "are white people's toy. White men like you."

Tanada flew into Josh like an eagle spearing a fish. She was all over him, and Josh toppled over on his back. She rode him to the ground like a bucking horse. All the while her fists were flailing.

"Take that back, you—you slave! I am not white man's toy and you know it. We should be friends. I am my own woman.

No man owns me. I work hard for my money."

The two rolled over and over. Keely was awake by then, and his first impulse was to separate them. But he let them go on. Whatever bothered Josh would have to come into the open if they were to live together for six months.

Tanada was stronger than Josh, who still hadn't recovered his full strength. She sat on him and punched until his face was bruised. Then she grabbed his nose between her thumb and finger and squeezed. Josh howled.

"Let go of my nose!" he demanded. "Let go!"

"Not till you take back what you said."

"Never!"

Tanada squeezed harder.

"Dang it all!" Josh said, using his worst cuss word. "That hurts."

"Too bad. Take back what you said."

"All right. You don't like whites either."

Tanada released her grip. Her face was hard, and Keely knew that he would never want her to get angry at him too.

"Do you know what he said about me?" she asked Keely.

"Yes, I think so."

"Not true." She stamped her foot angrily. "I am my own woman! Always!"

She dashed into the tent and emerged with her blankets.

"I will sleep over there." She pointed to a rock in the distance. "I will come back in morning—maybe." She glared at Josh. "Tlingit dog."

Keely spent an uneasy night. He hoped that Tanada was warm and that she wouldn't leave. She was a good hand and, besides, he admired her spunk. Still, there was nothing to keep her there. Nothing. And why was Josh behaving so badly? He decided it was time to confront Josh about Tanada.

"Most girls like her," Josh said, rubbing his nose, "are playthings of the whites." Then he added ruefully, "Maybe she is not."

But Keely sensed there was more, and suddenly it hit him. Josh was jealous.

"Hey," Keely said quietly, "you don't need to be afraid of her, Josh. You're my friend. You and I are alike. The world wants us and we don't want the world. We are brothers. Nothing will ever come between us."

"Not even this girl?"

"No."

"She's pretty."

"Yes, but you and I are friends for life, Josh. That's the way it is."

Josh grinned. "Am I being a fool?"

"Yes, you are, Josh."

The next morning Tanada returned. She cooked breakfast and afterward took up her ax as if nothing had happened, except for one brief exchange with Josh.

"I know," she said, "what is the matter."

"Oh?"

"You don't need to be worried, Josh. You and he are friends. I will not be first with him, I think." She glanced at Keely. "Anyhow, I don't know if I like him."

"Oh?"

"Pale skin is not very pretty."

Josh smiled. As Tanada smiled too, Keely's self-esteem took a dip. What was wrong with white skin? But he was relieved. The trouble had been brought into the open, and it had melted away.

The three worked fast and the cabin was

up in a week. Windows were a problem, because there was no glass.

"I will fix that," Tanada said.

She scraped elk hide to a thickness of paper. It was white and smooth.

"You don't see through this," she admitted, "but it lets light in. That is good."

There were two windows, one in Tanada's room and another in the main part of the cabin. The cabin was not a thing of beauty, with skin windows, a dirt floor, and a door of young pine poles. The logs had been chinked with grass and mud, and the roof was made of poles and dirt. When the heavy snow of winter dropped a couple of feet on them, though, they were inside. They were comfortable and dry, and the iron stove crackled.

And here we are, Keely thought, *three fugitives from life, making a go of it at the top of the world.* He found that he could think of worse things, such as Marcy, who would never again worry about good or bad things for eternity.

Chapter Nine

The snow deepened in proportion to the shortening days. The snow was a safeguard. Nobody would travel into the high country in winter, whatever his motives or objectives. Keely didn't underestimate Ivor Clatchett or Lyle Bolding. Neither man was a fool. And they knew about the waiting game, how it could nourish tensions that might make a man do dumb things. Blackax could be a problem because he'd lost both a slave and face with his people. But even that would not be enough to draw the chief or his braves into the bitter cold of the high mountains. Blackax would also bide his time, and his cunning mind would be at work.

The fact was, the snow was not only a protector but also a trap. There was no way Keely could escape. Escape in the high Olympics meant crashing through snow so deep that a twenty-foot pole would be lost. It meant facing winds of gale force and temperatures equal to those of Wyoming. He and his companions were stuck.

A shelter was built for Thorny and the packhorse to keep the wind from them. Keely remembered the previous winter all too painfully, when his stock froze stiff in the cold. He saw to it that the animals were well protected.

Aside from building the shelter, which didn't take long, there was little to do.

"You get me deer and elk," Tanada told the men, "and I will make you warm clothes."

Once supplied with her materials, Tanada worked long hours in the main room, warmed by the stove. She turned raw hides into soft, pliable skins. These she sewed into trousers and jackets for all three of them. Keely owned the best windbreaker that money could buy, but the buckskin jacket Tanada made was even better, and it cost nothing except labor. Tanada also shaped moccasins for them, and Keely's feet were warm for the first time that winter. Store-bought boots, oiled and slick, simply froze stiff in low temperatures. The dry-tanned moccasins of Tanada didn't freeze.

Keely had forgotten to buy one important item, a calendar. The days were marked off on a sheet of paper, every sixth day crossed to make seven. They spent what they thought was Christmas Day with songs of the season and a great roast of venison. On St. Valentine's Day Josh presented Tanada with a large wooden heart that he'd carved.

"You didn't think like that about me at first," was Tanada's wry comment.

"I change."

"Yes. You have changed."

"And you?"

"No. I am sorry, Josh Deerface. I am the same."

It was obvious to Keely that Josh had become interested in Tanada. And the fact of the matter was that he, too, began to take more than a casual notice of the girl. Her strength of character, her good humor, her willingness to do her part and more unlocked his heart. He had thought once that he would never get over Marcy, and he was disturbed about his feelings for Tanada. It seemed, somehow, disloyal.

Yet, human nature being what it is, his thoughts turned to Tanada. He realized that the two women were so different as to leave likenesses out of the picture. There were no similarities except in one respect —they were both their own people. Marcy had known what she liked. Tanada also knew what she liked. Both were strong women although their strengths lay in different areas. Marcy insisted on the more civilized offerings of life, and brought them into her life. Tanada's strength was based on earth things and what it took to get through another day.

A subtle competition began for Tanada's attention. It was started by Josh.

He returned late from a hunt one day.

"I got two deer down there." He pointed to a low valley. "Two shots," he added proudly with a furtive glance at Tanada, "two deer. I need the packhorse. Some of us"—he glanced at Keely slyly—"are good hunters. We keep meat on the table. Others sit around and don't do much."

Keely was amused...and ate the venison happily.

Josh made a snowman after a fall of fresh, wet snow.

"Indians do not do these foolish things," he explained to Keely, "but I see this snowman in white towns." He set the head on the round body. "But what I do, I do better. Is it not beautiful?"

He shouted the last sentence, so that Tanada, inside the house, looked out the door.

She nodded. "It is fair."

So Keely made a snowman twice as large and stuck twigs in its face for eyes, lips, and nose. Josh had not done so.

"Ha!" Josh exclaimed, seeing that he had been bettered.

"You have a snowman without eyes," Keely teased. "How can he see?"

"Bah!" Josh said in disgust.

Josh went outdoors in freezing weather, naked to the waist, to feed the horses. "Indians do not feel cold," he bragged. "Dark skin is tougher than poor, baby-white skin."

Keely went outdoors in his undershirt and bare feet to feed the horses the next day. He nearly frosted his feet, but he later said casually, "I would have stayed longer, but the horses told me to come in."

Josh said "Bah!" again but he examined Keely's feet with care. "Do not be foolish," he said. "You need feet."

"Who is a fool?" Keely asked.

The two men looked at each other, and suddenly they laughed.

Tanada, aware of what was happening, kept out of it. She wanted no trouble on her account and made a point of neutrality. But both men had grown dear to her. She had never known such kindness as given by Keely. She had never seen an Indian show off to a girl as Josh was doing. Both men touched her heart, but she remained aloof. She enjoyed and often sought the privacy of her room. There she listened to the men talking, and their talk often turned to spring and what must be done then.

"I think you should forget what you want," Josh advised Keely once.

"No, not on your life, Josh."

Tanada had never heard the white man's voice so harsh.

"It is dangerous."

"I don't care about that. You know it, Josh."

"I will help you fight, then."

"It's my fight. Don't risk your life, my friend."

"Ha!" The exclamation was a combination of irony and bitterness. "What kind of life do I have? Do I ever get back to my homeland? Maybe." Josh shrugged. "Maybe not. While I am here in this place, this is my home." He grinned. "You and she," he said, pointing to Tanada's room, "are my people. I owe you much."

"You owe me nothing, Josh."

Tanada didn't know about the Mossman murders at first. She didn't know about Marcy. Keely would never have told her, because the subject did not seem appropriate. Even with Josh he was reticent, but Tanada finally heard about the murders from Josh.

"So there was a woman," Tanada said quietly.

"Yes. And he is after the men who killed her."

"That good man! What sadness in his life."

"Yes, that good man."

"He will need help."

"He doesn't want it."

"He will need it."

"I am going to help."

Tanada nodded. "And me too."

"What can you do? You are a woman."

Keely was out, taking his turn at guard. Except in the most severe storms, they took turns. A high point a quarter of a mile away served as their lookout station. Keely was taking no chances.

The other two were alone in the main room of the house. Upon hearing Josh's disparaging remark, Tanada reached across the table at which they were sitting and grabbed his wrist. She twisted expertly and Josh flew from his chair like a windmilling scarecrow.

"Hey!" he hollered from the floor. "You're not supposed to do that."

"Well, I did. Now what do you think?" Tanada's eyes were hot.

"You are good," Josh admitted, rubbing his wrist. "Maybe you can help a man." He rose and put an arm around her waist. "I marry you and you make me fine squaw."

"And clean your fish, and cook your grub, and cut your wood?"

"Sure," Josh agreed heartily. "You make me a good wife."

Tanada removed Josh's arm from her waist. "One day you will find a woman from your own tribe."

About an hour later, returning to the cabin, Keely could tell by the thick atmosphere that something had happened.

"Trouble in paradise?" he asked.

"In where?" Josh wanted to know.

"Paradise."

"What is par-a-dise?" Josh pursued. "Whites have funny words."

"It is where the sun shines warm all the time and there is plenty of venison."

"She won't marry me," Josh said abruptly.

"Who?"

"Who do you think?" Josh made an impatient gesture. "We got lots of women here?"

"Oh."

"She good woman. I want her for my wife."

Tanada, who had been listening, interrupted. "Josh, I am not your slave. What a way to talk!"

Blushing, she went to her room and pulled tight the deerskin that served as a door.

"Sorry to hear that, Josh," Keely sympathized happily.

Josh looked at him closely. "By great god Raven," he whispered, "you like her that way too, eh?"

"Well, sure I *like* her, Josh. She is one of us. I like you too, you know."

"Yes," was the soft reply, "but not in same way."

Josh left, his eyes thoughtful. He and his friend had teased about Tanada's attention, but he had never dreamed that Keely could be serious. What whites—or Indians, for that matter—were ever serious about half-breed girls? Yet, he too, wanted Tanada. She was special and he knew it. He wanted her to be an important part of his life, and so did the man he admired most in the world. At that moment Josh was not happy.

Tanada did not play the game she could have. She could have pitted the two men against each other and made them jealous.

She could have used her power and become mistress of the camp. But she did not.

Tanada didn't play games. She didn't like them. She lived on a day-to-day basis, facing life as it called the turns. She was not cute or coy, and yet she wasn't indifferent. She was aware of her power, but she refused to use it. She respected the man who was avenging the death of people he had admired and loved. She respected his diving into a futile battle to save a drunk from he didn't even know what crime. He just hadn't liked the odds. And out of her respect grew liking, and out of liking a feeling of . . . Tanada was not sure how to name that feeling.

As for Josh, he amazed her. His diffidence was not the Indian way. Indian women, though they had power in a tribe, had few rights. They produced children, cooked, sewed, and worked at the menial chores while the men hunted and held council. Josh may or may not have been teasing about her cutting wood and other duties, but along with the teasing, if it was that, was a genuine friendship. Josh was thoughtful. He helped her in the house and even carried water for her on wash days—buckets of snow to be melted. That was woman's work in the tribes.

Tanada was confused. She liked Josh. She liked Keely. Perhaps she more than liked them and would have given her life for them without hesitation. For the first time she was respected and needed. It was a precious experience for a half-breed Indian girl who had never been respected or needed. If she had to choose, who would it be? She did not know.

The winter wore on. To keep from getting cabin fever, Keely and Josh made several overnight exploring trips. Tanada had the cabin to herself. And on two occasions Tanada went off by herself over the objections of both Keely and Josh.

"You'll freeze," Keely warned.

"You are a soft woman," Josh said. "There is no place for you in the high mountains."

"You are both wrong," Tanada replied with a laugh.

She not only went alone but on both occasions was gone for two nights while Keely and Josh fretted in the cabin. Both times Tanada returned with a packsack full of supplies that she had picked up in Blyn.

"You like kaupy?" the girl asked Keely. "Well, I bring you some."

"You could have frozen," Keely, who was nevertheless pleased, grumbled.

"And sugar for you," she added to Josh, who was also grumpy but pleased. He loved sugar in his coffee.

In the meantime, forces were moving into action that spelled trouble for Keely. Chief Blackax visited Ivor Clatchett. The chief intended to tell Clatchett without charge what he knew about Keely, but Ivor's attitude was so condescending and arrogant that it infuriated him, and he bartered the information for a quantity of tobacco and four knives. He returned to his village and called a council to relate his success.

"Now," he said, "white will fight white and I will be avenged for the stealing of my slave."

"Your plan is good," a member of the council agreed. "The tobacco is even better."

Though not exactly the words of praise

that he had hoped for, Chief Blackax had to settle for them. His plan would work, he was sure. Clatchett would take along plenty of men.

April arrived, bringing a warmer sun and melting snow. Keely increased his guard. He could not escape yet, nor could his stronghold be invaded, but he took no chances.

As the month dripped on, Keely found that he was watching Tanada more and more as a man watches a woman. Josh, too, felt his feelings increase for Tanada. Tanada felt the growth of emotion in both men, and she was more confused than ever.

By May the little camp, their haven in the high hills, was no longer the happy place it had been for many months. Human nature and the emotion of love had overtaken all three. A triangle formed, and though never spoken of and never revealed, it was there and it was felt.

Who, both men wondered silently, *will get the girl?*

Who, Tanada wondered, as she had before, *will I choose, if I choose either?* And she knew that she would have to choose one of the two men.

All three felt sadness and confusion, yet on the surface all three seemed the same.

It is an odd game, Keely thought, and so did Josh and Tanada.

Chapter Ten

It was Keely's tour of guard duty. He saw them coming, Ivor Clatchett followed by Jeeter and Morey. Bolding came next, and then a man Keely didn't know, probably a hired gun. Ivor wanted to be sure of his firepower. They were still a mile from the cabin when Keely first saw them, but they seemed to know just where they wanted to go. They were mounted and had crossed a ridge above Keely's outpost. They were heading for the forest below.

Keeping low, Keely ran for the cabin. A hot joy burned in his heart. The day of reckoning was here. He wouldn't have to go for them, after all. The killers of innocents had come to him. It was early May, nearly a year since the Mossman massacre, but the time was at hand.

He crashed through the door of the cabin with a savage grin lighting up his face.

Josh knew at once. "I get rifle," he cried.

"You don't have to, Josh. It's still my fight."

"I will fight too," Tanada declared.

"Ha!" Josh scoffed.

"I shoot better than you."

"Gun battle no place for woman." She retrieved her .25-20 rifle from the wall. "This gun holds ten shots." She looked at Keely. "Small bullets, but I kill bear with them."

Josh remained derisive. "You can't shoot mouse with that thing."

"This is not the time for arguing the merits of a gun," Keely interrupted, his voice as hard as the barrel of Tanada's rifle. "Tanada, I don't want either you or Josh in this. Stay out of it and you'll be all right."

Tanada gazed at him in disbelief. "All right? Are you crazy? We live with you all winter, me and Josh. Whites call that something—helping a criminal to escape. Whites put us in jail for that. Besides"—her dark eyes were fired up—"do you think Indians like Josh and someone like me will live to tell about this? Don't be dumb, Keely."

What Tanada pointed out was all too true. Certainly Ivor would leave nobody to tell tales. Certainly the white law would take a dim view of their living with a criminal should the pair survive. He nodded reluctantly.

"We won't wait in the cabin," he said. "They'd just set it on fire and we'd be killed like pigs coming out." He pointed to a copse of firs a hundred yards off. "We'll wait there."

They gathered their weapons quickly, along with the horses. Within ten minutes of Keely's arrival with the news, they were hidden and waiting.

"What next?" Josh asked.

"When they get close enough, start shooting."

"That is it?"

"What else?"

"I will go over there." Josh pointed to thick trees about fifty yards to their left.

"When you shoot, I do too. They don't know how many of us, see? Tanada, she go over there." He indicated another copse of trees to the right.

Keely saw the wisdom of the plan and nodded. "But," he said, "don't kill Ivor. I want him alive."

Tanada didn't argue, except to say, "But if he shoots at your back, then I will kill him."

Both she and Josh dispersed to their positions. They were no sooner settled than Ivor appeared at the edge of the forest. He and his gang had been following tree line for about a quarter of a mile and they were not exactly sure where Keely's camp was located. Keely could hear Ivor talking.

"I don't want mistakes this time, Jeeter. I want that fellow dead."

"And whoever is with him," Bolding added.

"Dead men tell no tales," Jeeter agreed, and cackled crazily. "Nor do dead women, either."

"It's just a rumor the half-breed is with him," Bolding said.

"Trust all rumors," Ivor snapped. "They can save your life."

"I want her if she's here," Bolding added with viciousness.

"Yeah, you're pretty good at killing ladies," Jeeter said with a guffaw. "Like that Mossman's wife."

The group stopped, facing the cabin at a distance of a few hundred feet. They were partially hidden by willows but Keely could make out their figures without too much trouble.

"Well," Ivor observed smugly, "it's just like Blackax told us. We got 'em."

"Yes," Bolding said. "Now what?"

Morey, who never had much to say, spoke: "You want I should knock on the door or somethin'? Mebbe ask fer tea?"

Jeeter guffawed again. "That'd be good. Then as you was sippin' tea, I'd fill them rascals with lead."

Ivor ignored his brothers. Instead, he called out, "You there in the cabin, can you offer some hospitality to a traveling preacher?"

When there was no answer, Ivor leveled his rifle and fired. With that, Keely fired his .44 at Ivor. But brush deflected the bullet and Ivor dived to the ground.

The peaceful mountains were suddenly

ablast with gunfire. Morey shot and Keely heard Tanada gasp. He fired at Morey and toppled him backward. Josh had started firing and Tanada was using her .25-20, and for a few moments lead split the sky like angry hornets.

When the firing stopped, while both sides reloaded and reassessed the situation, Keely crawled over to Tanada. She had only a slight wound, a skin cut, but it was bleeding a lot.

"Hurt?" he asked gently.

"Yes. You got him, I think." She pointed at the still form of Morey.

"Only four to go."

As he lay next to Tanada, whose blood stained the ground, an awful memory arose in Keely, a memory of the Mossman family lying in their blood. He saw Marcy again, lying so still, never to move again. He saw the Clatchetts and Bolding, their faces pinched with death-dealing, and he heard the screams of the children, Robert and Jackie. He heard the shots that stilled their voices forever.

Suddenly he stood up in plain sight of the enemy. He stood up, and in a red haze of anger and grief, he walked into the open.

"Let's get it over with!" he cried in a terrible voice. "Shoot! Shoot, you cowards!"

Shots came. And when they came, Keely fired back. He was aware that Josh and Tanada were doing the same as he. They, too, had risen from their shelters and were advancing. He saw Tanada aim a quick, cool shot and then saw Bolding collapse like a balloon whose air has been let out. He crumpled under the impact of the .25-20's small but ferocious slug and lay still.

Keely and his friends advanced as lead whistled around them. The hired gunman let out a screech and clutched his arm. Keely kept on, walking straight at Jeeter, firing again and again until Jeeter suddenly leaped up and clutched his leg.

"Ivor," he howled, "I'm hit!"

Keely threw himself on the man and they went down. As Jeeter's lank, bean-fed body hit the ground beneath his own, Keely felt an extreme satisfaction, an almost fiendish joy. He had the child killer and that child killer would not rise again.

He reached for his bowie knife, jerked it free of its sheath, and plunged the blade deep into the squirming figure. Jeeter gave a long, slow moan and opened his mouth to cry out, but blood choked him as he gyrated in a grim death dance. Eternity had met Jeeter Clatchett.

Keely felt a blow from behind, as if a hammer had struck him. He fell forward but sprang up immediately, knowing that he'd been hit by a shot. Ivor was now advancing on him, a satanic grin splitting his face. Ivor pulled the trigger of his rifle, only to have it fall on an empty chamber. Josh lifted his rifle and aimed, but Keely cried out, "Hold it! Remember, we want him alive!"

Josh held his fire and Ivor continued to live. He was the only one left alive except for the hired gunman. Lying behind a boulder, the gunman nursed a shattered arm as he wondered why he had allowed himself to get talked into such a mess. Ivor had said that the fight would be a cinch. He winced as his wound throbbed. This was no cinch.

Ivor, his eyes smoking with battle heat

and hatred, said, "What do you aim to do?"

"You just stand right there," Keely ordered. "Josh, shoot if he tries anything."

Josh nodded. "Please run," he invited Ivor. "Run, please."

But Ivor Clatchett did not heed the invitation. He glared, taking deep, shaky breaths.

Keely examined the others. Jeeter was dead, the knife protruding from his chest like a monument to evil. A slug in the left temple had ended Bolding's lawyering days forever. Morey's heart had been shattered. The hired gun lived, but he wasn't the least bit interested in more fighting. For all of them, it was over. Only Ivor was left.

Keely nodded toward the cabin. "Welcome to our humble home. I want you to see it."

Ivor did not budge. Keely went over and felled him with a blow to the jaw. Ivor flew up from the ground like a hawk, fists pumping, but Keely dropped him again. Ivor regained his feet, wobbly this time. "Why should I go in there?" he said. "You'll just kill me."

"We could do that here," Keely reminded him. "Now go."

"Why?" Ivor spat blood defiantly from crushed lips.

"Because I say so. Now move or I'll break you in half with pleasure."

Ivor moved, followed by the others. Once in the cabin, Keely produced a sheet of paper and a pencil.

"Now," he said, "I want a confession to the Mossman killings."

"I don't know what you're talking about."

"You wouldn't be here if you didn't. *Write!*"

"Nobody will believe it. They'll know you forced me to do it."

"How would they know that, Clatchett? They don't know what business you and I have, do they? *Write!*"

"You need witnesses to a confession."

"I have two." Keely indicated Josh and Tanada.

"An Indian and a half-breed?" Ivor sneered. "Everyone knows they'd sign anything for a pint of whiskey."

Josh stiffened and Tanada's eyes fired up.

Keely said gently, "Don't tempt them. *Write*."

Ivor wrote. He penned his entire confession in his magnificent scroll, down to the last detail. But when he finished, he seemed triumphant.

"A court will never accept and consider this confession, I tell you."

"I'm not worried about the courts." Keely's voice could have cut glass. "This will start the right people thinking about other disappearances." Keely's eyes bored into Ivor. "How did it feel to murder an entire family? Did you feel any compassion at all?"

"I didn't do it."

"Oh," came a voice from the door, "I think you might have had a hand in it."

It was Sheriff Williamson, who was accompanied by two deputies.

"Sheriff!" Ivor exclaimed. "What a coincidence. I want you to arrest these people for murder."

"This is no coincidence, Clatchett. After all, you did leave word at my office that you were after an outlaw—and you left instructions on just how to find him."

"Of course I did! I wanted the law in on this."

"Then you should have waited. But you didn't, because you wanted a dead witness before I arrived. You underestimate me, Clatchett. Tsk, tsk! What were you going to do—claim the killing of McGuire and these others"—the sheriff nodded at Josh and Tanada—"as self-defense? Then why did you hire the extra gun?"

"Now see here, Williamson, I demand that you arrest these hoodlums for killing my brothers and partner."

If Ivor Clatchett felt any cracks in his armor, they didn't show. He remained arrogant and indignant.

The sheriff didn't answer. Instead, he picked up Ivor's confession and studied it. Then he fished another paper from his pocket and unfolded it. He set down Ivor's confession and the paper on the table for all to see.

"The signature on this bill of sale is yours, Clatchett. No mistaking the handwriting. This is the Mossman sales document. How did you get such valuable land so cheap? Talk around Placer was that

Mossman had no plans to sell. Talk around there was that you tried to force him off."

Ivor's face remained stony, but his eyes narrowed to the slits of those of a trapped wolf.

"I think you have something to answer for, Clatchett," the sheriff went on. "Yes, sir, there's a lot of documents around with your signature on them. A lot of ground you bought up cheap in Placer, and a lot of timber here. People are missing, but if they aren't all dead, we'll find some who will talk."

Ivor's hand flashed. It held a stiletto, an ugly knife with a blade as sharp as a razor. He lunged at Keely, crying in a kind of howl, "I'll take you with me, McGuire!"

From the side, quicker than Keely could ever remember, swifter than the wind, Josh Deerface thrust himself between Ivor and Keely. The stiletto sank deep into the Indian's chest. At the same time, the sheriff's pistol thundered. Both men, Josh and Ivor, staggered and fell. Ivor was dead on contact with the dirt floor, but Josh still breathed.

Keely knelt beside him swiftly and cradled the dying man's head in his arms. "Josh," he murmured. "Why?"

"Friends do things for friends, eh?" Josh, a proud Tlingit, managed a smile. "You take Tanada now. She will cut you lots of wood...."

The voice stopped as life slipped away, a silent bird on the wing.

"Well, I'll be," Williamson muttered. He had seen friendship and bravery in his day, but never anything like this.

Tanada knelt beside the two men, her only friends, her loves, and circled them with her arms. A great and pervading silence engulfed the room, for all had seen death this day, and all had witnessed a noble act.

Chapter Eleven

Sheriff Williamson left the camp with the bodies of the slain strung over their horses. He did not take Josh Deerface, at Keely's request.

"I'll bury him," Keely said, "like he should be, and not in a pauper's grave."

The sheriff didn't care about that, but he did care about Keely.

"Don't leave the country," he directed, "without seeing me first. You're not in the clear until this confession gets to the authorities in Placer. I'll explain my investigation to them."

Keely nodded.

When they were alone, Keely and Tanada dug a grave in the rocky soil. They placed Josh's body inside it, along with his

179

rifle. This last was done at Tanada's insistence.

"Why the rifle?" Keely wanted to know.

Tanada looked at the white man with both the wisdom and superstition of those born to the wilderness and living by its rules.

"He may need it in the next world," she said.

Keely didn't argue the point. He was too grieved by the loss and how it came about. His question had been one of curiosity. If a dozen rifles would have benefited Josh Deerface, he would have buried a dozen with him.

After the burial, Keely and Tanada stood beside the grave quietly. Keely knew that words should be spoken, but he didn't know just what to say. He turned to Tanada. "Please, you speak. You know how."

Tanada raised her hands to the sky. "I have seen the death of a great man," she murmured. "May the spirits in his new world receive him with open hearts." Then she turned away.

"Is that all?" Keely wanted to know. He had expected a chant or, at least, a long eulogy.

"It is enough," Tanada said. "We will speak to him for all the rest of our lives. He will live in two worlds."

There was no need to stay here any longer, so Keely saddled Thorny and readied the packhorse, taking such provisions as would be needed for a long journey. Riding double on Thorny, who didn't take kindly to the weight, they left. They turned once for a last look at the cabin. The sun had come out and the place looked quaint, almost pretty, in the yellow rays. Josh Deerface's grave reflected the sun softly, and the mound seemed as settled as if it had been there forever.

"It is good," Tanada said. "He rests in peace. We go now."

They rode in silence for a way before Tanada asked, "What now?"

"As the sheriff says."

"And then?"

"And then?" Keely paused. "Well, Josh said I could take you now. Tell me, can I?"

Tanada smiled. "I think," she said, "that we three should spend our lives together. Yes, I will go with you. But where?"

"Back to my ranch, back to shortgrass country. With you there, I can stick it out." Keely returned Tanada's smile. Then he said, "I think you know that I love you. Shall we get married?"

"Yes," Tanada said, and a wave of joy washed over Keely.

Tanada reached around Keely's waist and gripped his hand. She held it for a long, long time, and she had never been happier in her life. *It is funny,* she thought, *how one can be happy and sad at the same time. But it is so.*